Ackno

There are so many people whose encouragement and support have kept me motivated. My husband Aidan, you have given me everything a writer needs – love, support, cups of tea, a listening ear, and unwavering belief in my dream. I am so lucky to share this with you.

My sister Jacqui, you will always be my light in the dark. My seat in the park.

To Isabelle and Ashton, thank you for getting me up early in the mornings. Without you I would not have reached this point so quickly. And to Isabelle, for picking the title when I couldn't decide, big kisses xxx.

To my editor, Rebecca Gumbley, for her excellent eagle eye, and to my book cover designer Nada Orlić, thank you for all your time and wonderful advice. For a newbie, I was so lucky to find two wonderful, caring individuals who have invested so much time and energy into my work.

My immense gratitude goes out to all those who have supported me through crowd sourcing, through morning teas, on Facebook and Twitter, you have all had a part to play in getting Lighthouse Love published.

Every person listed below made the dream of publishing my first book a reality, through my Pledge Me, crowd sourcing adventure.

My heartfelt thanks to you all!

Clare Allison*Sarah Diamond*Janet Elliot*
Douglas Elliot*Sue Ewart*Catherine Field-Dodgson*
Narina Foster*Jacqueline Graham*Tane Graham*
Karis Harland*Lydia Harris*Helen Joronen*Hannah Jones*
Cherie Kopilovic*Craig Larkin*Kristen Lunman*
Arran Milne*Wendy Milne*William Milne*
Heather Milne*Matthew Pender*Dallas Reeves*
Davina Smith*Maggie Sanders*Cheryl Thomson*
John Thomson*Caroline Toplis*

This is a work of fiction. Names, characters, places, and incidents are the products of the author's imagination. Any similarities to persons living or dead are purely coincidental.

Lighthouse Love
Copyright: Rochelle Elliot
Published 2013
Publisher Book Baby

All rights reserved. No part of this publication may be reproduced, stored in retrieval system, copied in any form or by any means, electronic, mechanical, photocopying, recording or otherwise transmitted without written permission from the publisher. You must not circulate this book in any format.

For Alison
Best Wishes
Rochelle Elliot
xxx

Chapter One

Lucy Dinsdale has only vague memories of the day she left Wellington, New Zealand. She was six years old and her father gave her a packet of wine gums, which her mother promptly confiscated. He'd patted her head, perhaps in the same way a dog-shy individual might do when told, "Come and pat Rover, he wouldn't hurt a fly."

Twenty-three years later, Lucy is back in the place of her birth. She joins the line to use her new passport for the first time, its black cover so different from the British red she holds in dual citizenship. She traces the engraved letters on its cover. *Aotearoa*, the Maori word for New Zealand. A memory of kindergarten plays on her jet-lagged mind as she shuffles forward in the queue. *Balls swinging on strings, what were they called?* She remembers the soft give of the balls, the crackle of plastic when she squeezed them in her hands.

"Poi, they're called poi!" Lucy says. A young woman looks up from her phone and smiles briefly before returning to her screen. *I have roots here,* Lucy thinks, *maybe this is where I belong?*

Though there is very little Lennon Taylor has managed to do for his daughter Lucy in the twenty-nine years of her life, he has made her adventure down under possible. She is very grateful for the bonus bonds he has bought in her name, every month since she was born. Her mother's unwillingness to take a cent of Lucy's father's money has left her with a hefty nest egg, plentiful enough to see Lucy through a few months of travelling, and, if she is careful, as her mother has insisted she be, a deposit on a house.

"Have fun, Lucy, but be sensible," her mother advised. "Save some pennies for when you're ready to settle down."

Settling down has proved elusive for Lucy. Her feet are in constant movement, and not only from her classical ballet training. While her daily dance classes have kept her active and agile, her metaphorical feet mirror those in her ballet slippers, pointing and sliding, twisting and turning, itching for the next movement. Lucy has always been a professional dancer. There has always been another show, another venue, another performance to prepare for. Ballet seasons and tours have given Lucy a structure of movement her whole life.

But last year, at twenty-nine years of age, Lucy stumbled on her life's path. She crashed and burned, and though the stage lights still burnt brightly, Lucy did not. She passed off her retirement from professional ballet on the back of recurring tendonitis which, though incredibly painful, was not really the reason she gave up on her old life.

I'm not going there, Lucy decides, shuffling forward again. She is desperate for distance from all that has gone before. She wants to wake up without a schedule full of rehearsals and performances. *I want to choose my own direction. To be someone new, someone different.*

The queue moves forward once again. *I'm on the other side of the world,* Lucy thinks, and then quickly pushes the thought away in case she is tempted to turn tail and buy a one-way ticket back to Britain. Lucy Dinsdale may appear brave, but she is still a tad apprehensive about where her new life might lie.

"You're young," her mother had said as Lucy lay on her couch, a hand draped dramatically over her eyes, her pale pink pyjamas in desperate need of a spin through the washing machine. "The world is your oyster! Get out there and enjoy it!" But facing such extraordinary freedom, Lucy had felt less pearl, and rather more pathetic. *Apathetic.* She felt too tired to trek, too old to Contiki.

"Don't be daft!" her mother had huffed, watching closely to make sure Lucy did not get chocolate on her cream cushions again. "You need to *do* something Lucy," her mother pushed.

"But I don't know what I *want* to do," Lucy had whined.

"Well you're not going to find out sitting in the snow in Kelso feeling sorry for yourself," Lucy's mother had replied.

Daphne Dinsdale was ever so slightly despairing of her only child, and a little anxious at the mess that grew daily in her semi-detached, modern home on the Scottish Borders. Her spacious clean lines and sea-green chaise longue had disappeared under a pile of magazines and biscuit packets. So mother had given daughter a wee prod and a little push, and in the hump between Christmas and New Year, Lucy felt compelled to form some kind of New Year's resolution.

"Why don't you have a holiday?" her mother had suggested over tea and toasted sandwiches at the Hazel Lodge Tearooms. "Why not go back to Ibiza? That James Blunt you like so much, he lives there. He's got a night club at the end of his garden."

"I know, Mum, I was the one who told you that," Lucy had replied.

"I thought I read it in *Hello*," her mother mused. "Anyway, what kind of man needs a night club in his garden? What's wrong with a few lemon trees and a nice pergola?"

"Let me get this right," Lucy had laughed. "You'd like me to go to Ibiza, find James Blunt, and suggest he swaps his pop star ways for growing lemons?"

"A few weeks of sunshine would do you good. You've been through a lot and you're still looking a bit pasty. A bit of vitamin D might perk you up."

"I think he lives in Switzerland now."

"I think you're missing the point," Daphne Dinsdale had sighed.

"I feel like I'd be running away," Lucy whispered back.

"Think of it more as changing tack," her mother suggested, "moving in a new direction. Storm's over now, Lucy, time to set sail again."

Lucy is shunted forward in the queue once again, her passport clutched to her chest, as if in prayer.

It's just that James Blunt is on his world tour, so there was only a slim chance he'd see me in a crowded place and would think I was so beautiful that he would dump his supermodel girlfriends and start writing songs for me instead. But New Zealand, well, New Zealand is my place of birth, so even though it is on the other side of the world, it feels a little less like running away, and little more like a journey home. Like that programme on the telly. What's it called?

Who do you think you are? Lucy?

"Hi-ya," the Customs man smiles at her. He checks her arrival card, "No food, plant or animal products?" Lucy shakes her head. "Welcome home," he says, and for the first time in twenty-five years, Lucy is a New Zealander.

"Nu Za-lun-da," she tries out her Kiwi accent as she waits for her bag to creak its way around the baggage belt.

Lucy finds the big orange airport flyer bus without a problem. She is to get off at the railway station, turn right and walk up Bunny Street, then left up Lambton Quay. *Up, up and away,* Lucy hums the tune. Her father will meet her at Astoria Café, beside Midland Park. He's found a window in his schedule, time to grab a quick bite.

"Hello sunshine!" she says as the bus pulls out into the traffic. Her eyes blink to adjust to the brightness. "Sunglasses!"

Lucy fishes in her bag for her phone, and opens up her notepad application. She starts a new list:

SPF30!

Bathers!

Sunglasses!

Chapter Two

Ethan James has a spring in his step. He marvels that the sun is so warm and the Wellington breeze so gentle, but then he knows you really can't beat Wellington on a good day.

Leaving his glass fortress of an office block behind, Ethan meanders along the waterfront, past the restaurants where fat cats discuss finance over crisp white linen, and women in oversized sunglasses sip wine from lipstick-stained crystal, twiddling their high heels under the tablecloths. It's after twelve, and the lunch hum is building.

"Not today, Gordon Ramsay. Another time, Heston." Ethan sails past on long hollow legs, his stomach rumbling.

He stops at the edge of the footpath. He closes his eyes for a moment in the bright midday sun and wishes he hadn't misplaced his sunnies. Ethan mentally runs through the places he might have left them while he waits for the lights to change so he can cross the road.

Georgie's car on Saturday morning?

I had them at the vege market.

The Southern Cross? I had them in the garden bar at lunch on Sunday.

The lights change to orange.

Orange! Oranges! Cricket practice on Tuesday night. They'll be in my cricket bag!

The traffic lights turn red, halting the cars in their tracks.

The little green man appears.

"Sign's out - cross now," Ethan calls out, making a couple of school kids snicker. Her hand is in the back pocket of his grey school shorts, and his hand sits just below her waist, where her school uniform skirt has been rolled a number of times. They cross the road together, and Ethan watches from behind, feeling a slight pang of longing for those easier days, when all that mattered was having enough money for a pie at the tuck shop, and whether Ruby Jones would get with him at the party on Saturday night.

Ethan strides up the street, welcoming the cool shadows of the buildings. He's desperately trying to remember the name of the girl he went out with in sixth form. *Sarah, Sandra? I'm sure it started with an S. Simone? Scarlett? Sally?* Ethan finds himself two shops too far and does a small U-turn. He sticks his head through an open door and waves at Penelope in the Nickity Nackity Nook.

"Lovely day, darling," she calls out to him, and he pauses for a moment in the door way, sucking in the smell of warm fudge, incense and lavender, a scent belonging only to the Nook.

"Off to the beach after closing, Penny?"

"Sand in me sandwiches? Not on your life, boy," Penelope says, while sorting the greeting cards into nice neat piles. She pauses to push her purple plastic-rimmed glasses up the bridge of her nose, from where they slip right down again. "A chardonnay on the deck and a bowl of salt and vinegar chips for me - I'll leave the surfing to you young things."

"You're not a day over twenty-one, Pen. I could give you a lesson."

"Get away with you," Penelope laughs, her cheeks turning pink, "I'm too old for that carry on." Ethan stands in the door way balancing on a pretend surfboard.

"Come on Penelope, give it a go," he winks. Ethan hasn't surfed a day in his life.

"Away," she says, "you'll be scaring off my customers!"

A girl with a heavy-looking backpack can't help but giggle. She has listened to the exchange while trying to decide between the mocha fudge and the caramel dream. Ethan sends a wink her way, though he can't quite see her properly through the metal display shelves. Then he waves goodbye to Penelope, who goes back to her stack of cards.

"Valentine's Day," Penelope tells the girl with the rucksack, who has decided on the caramel dream, "most young people these days wouldn't know Cupid if he bit them on the arse!"

Next door to the Nickity Nackity Nook, Ethan is where he was meant to be in the first place. He wouldn't say Burger Barn was his favourite spot in Wellington. Its industrial stainless steel seating is cold and impersonal, its exposed brickwork too obvious in its plastic falseness. Ethan thinks it's a soulless space, encouraging one to eat on the run. But all that aside, the 'Welly-in-my-Belly' is the best bloody burger he's ever tasted. And on a day like today he can zip in and out, and settle himself up in the park. He places his order and seven minutes later is rewarded with a brown paper bag, which he swings jauntily as he leaves the Burger Barn.

He jaywalks across Waring Taylor Street and strides into Midland Park. Ethan scans the grassy squares, the people perched on concrete edges, soaking up the sunshine. A small child covered in ice cream is chasing pigeons. A woman is handing out flyers for a jewellery expo.

"This way, E!" Ethan tries to locate the voice. "Over here, you big ol' giraffe!" Ethan's eyes fall on a patch of grass where Jamie is waving a pair of chop sticks in the air. "Plonk yourself down, young man. Glorious day it is. I see you've got the burger. I've been let out on a very tight leash and her there made me get something healthy." Ethan crouches down beside Jamie's wife Fran, who is stretched out on the grass, flicking through a magazine and grazing on a bunch of grapes and a punnet of strawberries.

"We had burgers last night," she says. "He can die of a heart attack after the house is finished." Ethan plants a kiss on the top of her head and steals a couple of grapes. "How's it going?" he asks.

"Carpet," she says.

"Shag-pile?" he suggests.

"That's why there are no boys on the carpet committee," she tells him. He takes a grape with a grin and sits himself down beside Jamie, who is layering thin slices of pickled ginger on circles of sushi. Ethan slides his burger from the brown paper bag and folds back the greaseproof paper.

"You're a bastard!" Jamie says, before placing a whole roll of sushi in his mouth. He chews twice, swallows, then moves to the next one. Ethan watches the people around him in various states of undress. He can feel the beads of perspiration forming between his shoulder blades.

"Quiz night," Jamie says, having cleared his tray of sushi, "Georgie is bringing that bloke."

"The one who thinks he's God's gift to rugby? He didn't even know where the next World Cup is going to be played."

"He knew the sponsor was Heineken," Jamie points out.

"He would, since he drank my last two bottles," Ethan replies.

"Bums on seats mate, you got a substitute?" Jamie asks, "We're still one down since Shazza left."

Ethan simply shakes his head, his mouth too full to answer.

"You heard from her lately? Sexy Shazza." Fran punches Jamie in the arm, without removing her eyes from a magazine story about three brown-haired girls in bikinis, frolicking on a sandy beach.

"Kardashians," Fran tells Ethan.

"Bless you," Ethan says.

"How's Shazza doing in Melbourne?" Fran asks.

"No idea, haven't heard from her since she left, but we didn't really keep in touch like that," Ethan mumbles through a mouth full of meat and bun.

"Shag and run?"

"Just a bit of fun," Ethan says, licking beetroot juice from his fingers.

"She's not on your Facebook, then?" Fran is pleased when he shakes his head. Shazza was always nice enough, but she thinks Ethan could probably find someone a little less... *loud.*

"Georgie's bloke it is then." Jamie says. "Seven-thirty – don't be late."

"Right on time, right, right, right on time," Ethan sings as Jamie pulls his wife up off the grass. They weave their way out of the lunchtime crowd, leaving Ethan to finish his burger alone.

It's not that he didn't find Shazza attractive. She was beautiful, well-groomed. *Not a hair out of place. Not a hair anywhere near where it usually is.* Ethan closes his eyes and lets his head drop to the left, then rolls it over to the right, stretching his neck.

It was good, quite titillating really. Put a new twist on quiz night, that's for sure. But then sometimes everything was so perfect, so overtly sexy and wanton, the chocolate body paint and the things she kept in her bedside drawer. Not that I'm complaining. He stares up at the clouds for a moment and thinks about Mrs Hass, his fifth form maths teacher with the hairy wart on her... *Yep, that'll do it!*

She was almost too perfect, Ethan decides. *I mean, once, I found myself looking for a stray hair, down there, anywhere!* He's not sure what he would have done if he found one.

"*A-HA!*" he imagines himself saying, "*I knew it!*" He chuckles, stuffing the wrapper from his burger back into the brown paper bag.

Ethan thinks, *Shazza was fun. A pleasant distraction. But I don't think my heart was ever really in it.*

Chapter Three

Lucy's heart beats rapidly. She has found Astoria and is sitting under a large white umbrella outside the buzzing brasserie, watching its waiters bustle by in crisp white shirts with black aprons tied around their waists. She is impressed with the spotless cutlery, the ice-cold water served in tall crystal goblets. The place, she reminds herself, is not important. She is here to see her father. It's about *family*. And hers is ten minutes late.

Lucy fiddles with her fork and smiles at a little boy who is happily shoving long thin French fries into his mouth while his frazzled mother takes large gulps of latte.

"Lucy?" A man in a suit takes the seat opposite her. He resembles the photo he emailed her a couple of years ago. Perhaps his hair is a little more salt and pepper, his face a little less springy.

"Dad!" she says, and though she would have liked to hug him, the table now prevents this.

"Your flight was good?"

"Yes, wonderful, shall we get coffee?" she asks, ready to signal the waiter.

"I'm afraid I can't stay," he says. "'Shanghai's having major problems with the design of the F3-AXRY and I've no choice but to hop on a plane this afternoon and sort it out." Lucy wonders for a moment what an F3-thingy is, but he continues talking.

"I've told them it's not on, that they can't just spring this on me, that I have plans." And for a moment Lucy feels outrage on both their behalves. They should realise that it's not every day your daughter flies in from the other side of the world!

"I mean, who's going to head the global alliance meeting next Wednesday?" he carries on, his eyes scanning the room before settling on a spot somewhere above her head. "It's a complete balls-up."

"Right," Lucy says, and smiles brightly, though she is not sure why.

"Now I'm sure you've got a million things planned, I'm not sure what OEs are like on this side of the ditch, but I'm sure you'll be bungy jumping every other weekend. Do you have enough? Money, I mean. I can put a transfer through this afternoon if you..."

"No," Lucy rushes in, "no, I'm fine... lots of money."

"Well, if you're sure. I'd better run – shall I email you when I get back? We could try again."

"Sure, yes, that would be good." Lucy watches him stand up. His grey suit looks expensive, his pointy shoes are so well polished, Lucy is sure if she bent down close she would see her reflection in them. His phone rings, and he answers it.

"Okay Jill, the three o'clock afternoon flight will have to do. Well if you can't get business class just book first – the bastards can pay for it." He smiles and winks at his only daughter, a light pat on her arm, and then he is gone.

Lucy is not sure what to do. She collects her backpack from behind the front desk, steps out into the sunshine and melts into the lunch crowd. She chooses a concrete ledge in the park, where she thinks she will sit for just a moment. She was expecting to stay with her father. *He didn't even ask where I was staying.* Lucy focuses on the facts. She has the *Lonely Planet* guide and knows she can hop on the yellow bus to get to a hostel. She has plenty of money, and now she has plenty of time.

But Lucy has never been very good with maps. She has tapped into the mapping app on her phone, and found the street where she thinks she is, but it still doesn't make sense. *If I make it bigger I can't see where I'm going. If I make it smaller, I can't see the street names. Where is Courtenay Place?* If she can get there, she can get to a hostel. And a pub.. She lets two fat blobs of water fall from her eyes onto the hem of her white T-shirt. Then she stands up straight and starts walking.

Ethan would have been happy to help; he is quite good with a map. But Ethan is walking in the other direction. Throwing his brown paper bag in the rubbish bin, he waits for the lights to change, then walks down Lambton Quay, hoping he'll have enough time to stop in at the chemist for a quick spritz of cologne before his meeting.

Lucy chooses to ask a short man in brown cords, who takes the phone from her hand and shows her how to tap in her location and her destination. Two red flags appear on the screen and Lucy thanks the man profusely. He points out the bus stop, and instructs her to get off at the Embassy Theatre.

Less than an hour later, Lucy finds herself at a hostel that is neither too basic nor too fancy. She is tired and not much in the mood for sharing a dorm, so she pays for a private room.

"Awesome," the young bloke at the reception desk says, taking her details and putting her credit card through the machine. Lucy can't stop staring at the lizard tattooed on his forearm.

"Tuatara," he explains, "world-famous here in *En-Zud*. Take the stairs, babe," he says, "down the hall on the left. Press the red button if you're back after midnight. Don't forget your swipe card. Great day to get out and about, babe, you much of a swimmer? Oriental Parade'll be packed this arvo. Grab a Trumpet and you'll be okey-dokey, hokey pokey," he says, raising his eyebrows and smiling. Lucy nods, not willing to admit she has no idea what she would need a trumpet for, let alone if she wants to be hokey pokey. She climbs the stairs and wanders down the narrow hall way, checking door numbers against the one on her card.

Forty-nine - just in time, Lucy thinks, as she slides her card into the door and pushes her way into the room. She lets her rucksack pull her backwards onto the bed, where she stays for a moment, staring up at the white ceiling.

Perhaps I was expecting too much. I know that's what Mum will say when I get up the courage to call her. That she had tried to warn me. She will say I need to find my own way, that no man - father, husband or boyfriend, will ever be able to give me something I can't find inside myself.

Wriggling from her pack, Lucy decides she is pleased with her room. It is light and airy. The window has been left ajar, and pulls in the sounds of the afternoon traffic. It makes her feel less alone. There is a television she doesn't bother turning on. She pushes her pack over to make extra room, and lies beside it on the double bed. She thinks maybe a walk in the sunshine would be nice, but her eyelids are heavy, matching the feeling in her heart and the pit of her stomach. So she closes her eyes and goes to sleep.

Chapter Four

On the other side of town, it's been a very good afternoon for Ethan James. His progress report was met, on the whole, with resounding approval. Just one or two niggles, a bigger bathroom space here, a wider entranceway there, and they were still a way off settling on the screening for the upstairs landing. But these are baby problems in the big scheme of project management, and Ethan believes things are coming together nicely.

He whistles happily as he waits for the lights to change, his Jamie Oliver-esque scooter humming beneath him as he zips around the Basin Reserve and up over the hill, down to Island Bay, where he zig-zags through the streets, and squeezes into the garage beside Georgie's Corolla hatchback.

I'm really enjoying this project, Ethan thinks, as he starts climbing the eighty-two steps up to his home on the hill. *Really, really enjoying it. I always thought the sheer size and brilliance of organising a big build – the magnificent giant skyscraper – was what it was all about. But these clients are bloody great, and their home, when I'm done, is going to be fantastic.*

But the job in Dubai – the one he's been working towards since trade school, since tech, since university – is fast approaching.

Do I still want it? Ethan asks himself. He pauses for a few deep breaths around the forty-ninth step. *Course I bloody well do! It's Dubai!* He looks out across the houses of Island Bay, across the rocky shore and out to sea, where the ferry sails across the skyline. *It's a dream job, isn't it?* He keeps marching upwards, under a canopy of punga branches that grow across the seemingly endless steps.

"Come on, E," Georgie calls over the gate. His flatmate is un-pegging the towels he hung out that morning, rolling them into balls and shoving them in the basket at her feet. He waits a moment for his breath to catch up with him.

"Haven't I told you that if you fold them at the washing line, it's one less job?"

"Right you are, Martha Stewart!" Georgie winks, rolling up another one and shoving it in with the others. "Quiz night is off, all summer apparently," she yells after him as he disappears into the house. "But they've got Smashed Apples playing tonight, so we're still going in!"

Ethan goes straight to the fridge, before he remembers the lack of cool beverages.

"Your man owes me two beers!" he grumbles as Georgie appears through the door.

"Absolutely," She smiles and blows him a kiss as she walks past with the washing basket. "I grabbed some chicken and coleslaw on the way home," she calls down the hallway, "You get changed, I'll serve up."

They sit under the clothesline as the sun slowly edges behind the bush, dappling their faces with evening light. Their blue plastic chairs are warm from an afternoon baking in the sun's rays. With dinner plates balanced on their knees, Ethan and Georgie fork food into their mouths and mop up coleslaw dressing with bits of bread taken straight from the bag that rests at Ethan's feet.

"So, this bloke..." Ethan says, between mouthfuls.

"Felix."

"What, like the cat? Is that his real name?" Ethan asks.

"Well, I think so." Georgie slaps and scratches at a sand-fly on her leg, then puts a forkful of chicken in her mouth and chews thoughtfully. "He's really honest, you know? It's kind of refreshing. If he wants to see me, he calls, any time, day or night. And he's just honest about it." Ethan thinks, *Booty call,* but holds the thought inside his head. He nods and fills his mouth with bread and coleslaw.

"So, you love him?" he mumbles through his mouthful. Georgie screws up her face and shrugs.

"I really think we've got something good, you know? He doesn't expect me to be anything I'm not, and vice versa. You get what you get, and you don't get upset."

"Right," Ethan smiles. He's not so sure having such low expectations is a good thing. He's not sure Felix is such a good thing, not where Georgie is concerned, but he doesn't really feel it's his place to say anything.

What would I say anyway? Ethan wonders. *"Hey Georgie, your boyfriend is a dickhead?"*

Ethan is happy to drive Georgie's car into town. He's got an early breakfast meeting tomorrow, so he'll only be having a couple. Georgie, on the other hand, has a big night planned. A long weekend away from her desk in the marketing department at Buzz FM. Felix, who fills the late night DJ spot at the same radio station, has three days off as well. Georgie knows because she has checked his roster. They drive via Hataitai to pick up Felix, Georgie running in to collect him while Ethan sits double-parked outside.

"Hey man, good to see you." Felix says, taking the front passenger seat. Ethan smiles and notes the number of leather and metal bracelets around Felix's wrists. He isn't sure he trusts a man who wears more jewellery than his mother. Felix immediately starts fiddling with the stereo, and Ethan fights the urge to slap away his hand, with its silver skull ring and strange tattooed letters in a language Ethan can't read.

"Great tunes." Felix is shuffling through Ethan's iPod. "Jefferson Starship, eh? You know they still play that on The Breeze?" He winks at Georgie in the back seat and she giggles. *God, he's wearing eyeliner*, Ethan thinks.

They enter the Mount Victoria tunnel, and Ethan returns a cheerful toot-toot from a passing motorist. Neither Ethan nor Georgie mention their many drunken nights listening to *Love Songs till Late* on The Breeze. Ethan doubts Felix would see the humour in it.

Chapter Five

Lucy wakes up a little hazy and a lot hungry. She digs in her backpack and finds the caramel dream fudge she bought for her father, stuffing two pieces in her mouth while she strips off her clothes. Though slightly suspicious of the aged shower cubicle, with its 1970s lime-green and brown tiles, the jet of water is strong and Lucy soon feels her body wake up.

She hasn't unpacked her towel, so she drips into the bedroom and unzips her backpack. She pulls out her towel, then digs around and finds a fresh bra and knickers, her skinny jeans and a white T-shirt. She loops a pale blue scarf around her neck and lets a pile of knickers and vests fall to the floor as she pulls her silver ballet flats from the bag. She spreads the contents of her make-up bag across the small bedside table and sets about sponging on foundation. She adds a slick of eyeliner and a layer of lip gloss, the tube of which she stuffs in her white tote bag, along with her wallet, her passport, her phone and her room card.

At reception, the friendly bloke with the tuatara tattoo has been replaced by a young man wearing sunglasses, whose interest in customer service is small. He informs Lucy it's past eight-thirty, so dinner's over, but there's a pub down by the waterfront that does bar food. He yawns and nods towards the door, "Beside Te Papa, the big museum. Turn left and keep walking."

Lucy does as she's told and keeps walking until she hits the harbour. She would like to join the other people who stroll past in the warm evening air. She thinks Wellington quite beautiful and stops for a moment, as the dusky natural light fades and the lights from the city twinkle brightly on the water. But she's hungry, starving even, and chooses to follow the sounds of chinking glass and cheery voices, into the waterfront bar.

Lucy orders at the bar, foregoing the Caesar salad she thinks she should be having in favour of the wedges, loaded with bacon, cheese and sour cream. *I need the carbs for energy to fight off the jet lag,* she decides. She finds a stool at a small, high table, squeezing in and digging around in her handbag, looking busy while the table's previous occupants don jackets and organise themselves for their departure. She sips from her small glass of white wine and settles in, joining her fellow patrons watching cricket on a large flat-screen. The yellow team appears victorious over the blue team, and the room erupts in cheers. Lucy's wedges arrive, and she tucks in.

A young couple ask Lucy if she minds them joining her, and Lucy smiles warmly and welcomes them. She tells the woman she is from England, that it's her first day in New Zealand.

"Cool," the orange-lipsticked mouth replies with a tight smile, then the girl retrieves her phone from her bag and doesn't look up from it again. Her partner stares intently at the television screen, listening to sweaty cricketers talk about their innings.

Lucy plasters a bright smile on her face and desperately tries to think of something interesting to say. But the woman stands a minute later, eyes still glued to the screen on her phone,

"Come on, they're there now, I don't want to miss the start," she moans, waiting impatiently as her partner gulps back his pint. "Thanks," she waves distractedly, and Lucy tries not to feel too dejected. Her smile falters. The polished table lies empty before her. Lucy tries to think of herself as part of the buzz around her, but a crowded detachment smothers her senses and leaves her disorientated.

The television is turned off. A voice squeaks on a microphone that the band will start in half an hour, and Lucy thinks perhaps she'll just finish her wedges and offer up her seat to someone else.

Ethan, Georgie and Felix meet Jamie and Fran in the car park. They tumble into their favourite pub, their loud and confusing conversations overlapping and intersecting.

"*Shagging*? At six in the morning?"

"I swear..."

"Heel broke right off. I took them straight back."

"It was the third over..."

"I thought I'd put them in my cricket bag."

"Can you *see* the bruise on my thigh? Look."

"He looked right at me. Like, I didn't know what to do."

Lucy knows she shouldn't stare, but their bubbling

conversation and excited chatter is endearing. She tries to follow their conversation. It sounds like someone has been playing cricket in red high heels, and that one of them has found their sunglasses on the back seat of a car that was being used for some other person's extracurricular activities.

"Shagging? Like, real shagging?"

"They didn't have the red in my size. Tried to get me to take the purple. I told them to fuck off, I want red!"

"Bollocks it was wide!"

"Yep, full-on shagging."

"They're ordering them in for me."

Jamie looks around, trying to find a spot they can all fit into. He makes eye contact with a small, pretty girl sitting alone at a table with an empty wine glass. Lucy smiles back at the tall man with the fluffy beard and decides to be brave.

"You can sit here," she shrugs.

"Wicked!" Jamie gives her a thumbs-up, then turns to the others. "We're sitting here with this fine human being. Best behaviour now, everyone, let's make a good impression." Bar stools scrape against the polished concrete floors, and handbags are pushed under the table.

"I'm Fran. The tall caveman is my husband, Jamie. He thinks the beard makes him look sophisticated, when really he looks like a knob. But the more I tell him, the longer he'll keep it. I'm having a cider, do you like cider?"

Lucy nods and Fran yells over the crowd, "Oy, Ethan, get the girl a cider as well." The one called Ethan waves over his shoulder without turning around,

"Lucy," Lucy says, offering her hand to Fran.

"Great to meet you, I'm Felix," a smooth voice croons. Felix slides his hand across the table and into hers. Lucy tries to smile. The hand is slightly sweaty, and holds on for a moment too long.

"I'm Georgie, and this hunk of spunk is mine." The girl with the black hair and the white blonde fringe starts kissing the guy named Felix ferociously. Lucy wonders where exactly she should look. She settles on Fran, who sticks her fingers in her mouth and pretends to gag.

And then Lucy meets Ethan. She watches as he carefully carries two pints of cider and a pint of lager from the bar to their table. He slides in the small gap between Lucy and Fran and Lucy can feel the warmth of his body through his blue chequered shirt.

"Get a bloody room, you two!" he says, flicking foam from his pint glass across the table. Georgie laughs and pokes her tongue out, but the Felix bloke looks less than impressed.

"I'm going for a fag," he says.

"He's a knob," Ethan whispers in Lucy's ear, "but don't tell Georgie I said that." He extends his hand, and in contrast to Felix's sweaty one, Ethan's is firm and cool in Lucy's own.

"Pleased to meet you," Lucy says.

"Likewise," Ethan smiles.

Lucy sips her cider and answers the group's questions of how and who and where.

"Alone! On the other side of the world," Fran marvels. "God, you're so brave! I'd probably be hiding in my hotel room. You stick with us, babe, we'll look after you!" And when Lucy feels Ethan's hands gently touch her shoulders as he squeezes past her on the way to the bar for another round, she thinks that sticking around might be quite nice. She misses the nudge Fran gives Georgie, and doesn't hear Jamie whisper, "Shazza who?" in his wife's ear, before he announces he's "off for a slash," much to Fran's embarrassment.

"He's still in training," she explains to Lucy, who doesn't seem to hear her. She's busy watching Ethan at the bar. Her eyes light up when he returns to the table. Fran and Georgie take a moment to wiggle eyebrows at each other, noting the extra colour in Ethan's cheeks, the way he leans into Lucy when she speaks, the way he runs his hand along his jawline, as he always does when he's nervous.

Jamie returns from the loo and an argument erupts over cut or loop pile.

"Fran and Jamie are doing up a house," Ethan explains, "it's carpet this week – last week it was bathtubs."

"And the week before that it was light switches," Georgie pipes up, "bloody boring."

"But imagine at the end," Lucy enthuses, "having something you've created, something solid and everlasting."

"Exactly!" Fran nods. Ethan smiles and holds Lucy's gaze till she blushes and gets very busy watching the band set up on the stage in the corner.

"Big one this Sunday," Jamie yells across the table.

"We've just made it off the bottom of the table with one game of the season left," Ethan explains.

"Ethan here whacked a six off the last ball on Sunday."

"Lucy doesn't care about your silly cricket game," Fran says, "it's social grade, you're not in the bloody Black Caps."

"They spend more time in the clubrooms than on the field," Georgie laughs, straining her neck to see if Felix has come back inside from his latest smoke.

"Strategy meetings," Ethan whispers in Lucy's ear, lightly tapping her hand with his own.

"She may be pretty," Jamie points at Lucy first, then Ethan, "but don't you be giving away our winning plans. You've only just met her – she could be a spy sent from the opposition!"

"I can't see the Khandallah Camels spending their beer money on a Bond girl," Georgie laughs. And Lucy, though she has no idea who the Khandallah Camels are, laughs along with the good-natured banter.

Conversation crashes to a halt when the band starts up. The three blokes on stage play a mix of old classics and loud, head-bashing originals that send a sea of teenage girls into a hand-waving trance. The dude on the guitar seems more interested in his musical instrument than the hormones before him, keeping his eyes closed, or staring zombie-like at the back wall of the pub. The lead singer is more forthcoming, stepping into the crowd now and then, proffering his mic for the brave tone-deaf masses to carry the lyrics for a moment. The third member appears to hold the show together, changing with ease from drums to keyboard to guitar. A harmonica makes an appearance at one point, as does a bongo drum, which one lucky girl gets to climb up on stage and have a go on.

"Brilliant musician, that guy," Ethan says to Lucy when the band stops for a break. "I wouldn't be surprised if he gets out a recorder in the next half."

"I was thinking the triangle, or maybe those clicky things I used to play at school."

"Castanets?" Ethan asks, making his thumbs and fingers into moving bird beaks, and making Lucy nod her head enthusiastically and say, "Yes, yes, those things!" Ethan would quite like to hold Lucy's hand about now, but the moment is lost when Felix and Georgie's voices rise above their own.

"I'll come with you, then. You've spent half the night out fagging."

"Loosen the leash, *darling*." An unmistakable drunken slur is clear in Felix's voice as he stumbles off outside again. Georgie fills the awkward moment by sculling the rest of her drink.

"Off to the loo," she smiles.

"Don't know what on earth she sees in him," Fran says, dabbing on lip gloss and digging around in her handbag for her cell phone. "We're off home," she tells Ethan, giving him a peck on the cheek and doing the same for Lucy. "It was really cool to meet you. Give Ethan your number, we'll hook up again!" she winks.

"Fred Flintstone," Fran calls to her husband, "your ride is leaving."

"Yabba dabba doo! I never turn down an offer like that,"

Jamie says, rubbing his beard. Then he lifts Fran off the ground in a bear hug.

Ethan turns to Lucy.

"Do you want to stay for part two, or do you fancy a bit of fresh air?"

They sit outside on large grey metal balls that are bolted to the wharf a short distance from the pub. The music pumps in the background, a song that Lucy doesn't know but Ethan hums along to. Each ball is a good half-metre apart from the next, and though Ethan would like to move closer to Lucy, he reluctantly realises that one ball is too small. Instead he tells her he's a project manager in the building industry, and he talks about the waterfront development, the art along the walkway, the buildings that have risen from derelict sheds, and the Sunday fruit and vege markets.

Lucy likes the sound of his voice. Her body remembers his warmth from inside the bar, and she also thinks about moving closer. But the balls are too damn small. She could sit in his lap, she supposes, *but how awkward that would be!* So she listens to his voice and to the water moving beneath her. To her heart hammering. She tells him she is a dancer. *Was* a dancer. Ballet. That she was professional, before tendonitis turned her into a has-been. She doesn't mention the other stuff. It's not the time or the place.

"I can still dance," she explains, "just not professionally, and not day-in and day-out with no downtime." Ethan thinks he would like to see her dance. He tells her he has lived in

Wellington most of his life. He was born 'up north' and won his first baby photo competition aged nine months.

"I embarked on quite a successful child modelling career: Marmite, Pineapple Lumps, toilet paper."

"I'm impressed," Lucy says.

"It was cut short in eighty-seven, though," Ethan continues. "The All Blacks won the World Cup. I was seven and refused to miss a single training session or game on my road to achieving All Black glory. Then I lost all four of my front teeth in the space of two months. Career ending."

"And your All Black dream?" Lucy asks.

"Still working on that one – maybe 2015 will be my year."

Lucy likes that he uses his hands a lot when he talks. She tells him she was born in Wellington too.

"Breaker Beach I think?" she ventures.

"Breaker Bay," he corrects her.

"Then when I was four my mum and dad split up, and my mum and I went back to Britain. We lived with my gran in Kelso – it's down the bottom of Scotland," she explains. "And when my ballet took off, we moved to London."

"Country living to city slicking," Ethan says, his foot tapping to the beat of the music from the pub behind them.

"I guess so," Lucy laughs. "Gran had chickens and a few sheep and a vegetable garden the size of a swimming pool. My mother lives back in Kelso now, but she prefers to get her eggs from the supermarket, and her salad in little plastic bags."

"And what about you?" Ethan asks.

"I've been living in London with my best friend, Liz. She's still dancing. She owns a small flat on Kilburn High Road." Ethan has only been to London once, when he was twenty, and he had spent most of his time at a pub called the Strong and Mighty, which he and his mates called the Old and Flirty, due to the patrons they found there. Lucy laughs when he tells her this, but is quiet when he asks, "What brings you down under? Are you here for the long haul?"

"I don't really know," Lucy shrugs. "I wanted to see my dad, and have a bit of an adventure. As for what I want to 'do with my life,'" Lucy uses her fingers to put the words in inverted commas, "I feel like I'm a ballet has-been," she muses, "but I'm not sure what I could-be. Or where I will be, once I do figure it all out."

Ethan would like to say he'd be interested in discussing what would-could-be, or if he might-be able to interest her in moving off the silver balls, and over to the wooden seat he's been eyeing up, by the bridge. But Lucy is staring out to sea, lost in thought, and it doesn't seem right to disturb her. A soft brown curl blows gently across her cheek and he longs to lean over and tuck it behind her ear. But the distance is too far. He estimates she is about twenty-five centimetres out of arm's reach.

"Home, James!" a voice calls, and Ethan and Lucy turn to see Georgie holding Felix up beside her. Or is it the other way around?

"Bloody great," Ethan murmurs under his breath, and they both stand, Lucy picking up her tote bag, and Ethan putting his hand in his pocket, then pulling it back out with a set of car keys. Lucy's smile meets Ethan's eyes. Then she yawns, a long wide unstoppable yawn that exposes her small pink tongue, and a single filling in her rear molar. She clamps a hand over her mouth.

"God, I'm sorry, it's been a long day," she says.

"Jet lag?" Ethan asks. Lucy nods and stretches to ward off the tiredness.

"A ride?" he asks.

"I'm just up there," Lucy says, pointing in the general direction she had come from earlier in the night.

"Still, it's late. You're tired. The car is just over there. In the Te Papa car park."

"If you're sure?" Lucy asks.

"If you don't mind the drunken ones?" Ethan replies. Lucy doesn't mind.

"Come on then," he says, casually reaching out and taking her warm hand in his own.

Lucy feels herself floating, and not just from the cider and the jet lag.

Chapter Six

Lucy wakes slowly, letting the sounds of the morning wash over her. The screen on her phone says it has only just gone seven, so she buries herself under the pillow and drifts, sifting through the memories of the night before.

She likes how Ethan's hand had fitted around her own, and thinks his hair was a sort of dusty blonde, and his bottom two teeth overlapped just slightly, and his eyes were...

Lucy feels her stomach fill with butterflies; a wave of nervous excitement makes her giggle and wriggle in her bed. She pulls the white sheet up over her face and stretches her legs out long, making pretend snow angels on the mattress.

There is a new energy about Lucy, something – or someone – has her wired. She has little choice but to sit up, get up, and get going.

A quick shower, a fresh T-shirt and she is on her way. She walks for a bit, settling into the pace of the other morning movers, watching them head off in pursuit of their daily activities: gym shoes and sweat bands; high heels and briefcases. Down and around the corner, on Courtenay Place, she finds a café that is open for breakfast. The formica tables and squishy chairs are chipped and worn, giving the café a lived-in feeling, and Lucy is soon crunching on toasted muesli and organic Greek yoghurt.

She fishes out her phone and sends a quick text to her

Mum, just to say she has a hostel and a happy day of sightseeing planned. Then she switches it to silent.

Where yesterday Lucy may have welcomed a debrief on her disappearing dad, a pep talk on passing up the past in favour of future possibilities, today she does not want to talk to anyone. Today she wants all to herself, to do as she wishes without anyone peering over her shoulder or wondering what she's up to. She does not want to share her plans.

Because Lucy knows exactly where today is leading, and how she's going to get there. She takes a dusty sugared doughnut and a latte to go. The clouds are thicker today, and the breeze a little cooler. Licking sugar from her fingers and sipping the last of her latte, Lucy sets off to get lost.

A morning at Te Papa is where Lucy settles into New Zealand. She rides in a waka, survives an earthquake and gets lost in the *Golden Days* exhibit, trying to remember the toys from her childhood.

Did I ever own spokey dokeys? Or just hanker after them? I know I owned a bunch of My Little Ponies, though I couldn't say where or who they came from, or where they went.

In the gift shop she spends a long time reading a picture book about funny tummy animals that make you feel nervous when you're going somewhere new. A gaggle of geese and a flutter of butterflies, having a party in your stomach.

"That's just how it feels," Lucy whispers. She puts the book back on the shelf, choosing instead to buy an 'I Heart Wellington' badge. She exits the museum, leaving a trail of fluttering butterflies behind her.

Lucy plans to wander the waterfront, but the weather isn't much to write home about. She wraps her cardi tight around her body and, like the others around her, she hustles quickly, her soft curls of hair whipped in every direction. Past a playground, a pile of kayaks and a rock-climbing wall. She stops a woman dressed head to toe in lycra, who jogs on the spot and offers excellent directions to 'the shops'.

The Museum of City and Sea is right where the lycra lady said it would be. Lucy marches across the road, takes a right, then a left, and finds she is back where she was the day before. Midland Park is sparsely populated today. Only a hardy few are willing to embrace the chilly breeze. People in business suits stride confidently along Lambton Quay, clear plastic trays of sushi swish past under Lucy's nose, and the smell of a cookie shop is intoxicating.

But it is Kirkcaldie and Stains, the big old department store, which entices her in. And the moment her feet touch the wide spiral staircase, Lucy is whisked back through the decades. She stops for a moment with her hand on the rail, and remembers the feel of her black patent leather shoes, the itchy bite on her knee under her pale pink tights, and the pink and white candy-striped dress that billowed out when she twirled around. Her hair had been in pigtails, to hide the large chunk she had cut out of it the week before. There were birds in a giant cage and a piano playing somewhere in the shop. Though little Lucy had wanted to linger by the birds, her mother had seen her father waiting at the café and had hurried her along. He had already chosen for her and, at six years old, Lucy had blinked fast to stop the tears at the injustice of such decisions being made without her approval.

"Ham sandwich first," he'd demanded, but when he wasn't looking, she had stuck her finger deep into the neenish tart and sucked off the sugary chocolate.

Grown-up Lucy has always been amazed that such memories could exist unnoticed in her mind, until something came along – a smell, a taste, a sight; only then would they would bob, like corks, back up to the surface. She climbs the remaining stairs and wanders through the shoe and handbag displays, getting lost in the fancy furnishings, and finally ending up at a café that could be the one from her childhood but, there again, might not be. She orders a pot of English Breakfast tea, which seems suited to her surroundings, and a cheese scone that she smothers with butter and jam and cuts into bite-sized pieces, the way her gran always did and her mother still does. She sits up high on a stool and watches through the window as the world passes by.

Perhaps this could be my home, Lucy thinks. *I certainly feel connections here. There are memories here that belong only to me. But there again, remember when I danced in the Penzance Pantomime in England? Did I not wander the streets, reliving my childhood holidays, licking ice creams on the pebble shore and chasing the Thomas boys who rented the holiday cottage next door to our own? Maybe I belong there as much as I do here?*

Lucy works her memory hard, pulling up pictures in her

mind's eye of a pink bedspread and wallpaper covered in yellow roses. Kneeling up on a chair while eating Weetbix and warm milk. A large brown couch with an orange cat, who growled in warning when she got too close. But the pictures were faint and faded around the edges, making Lucy question whether she remembered such things, or if they were simply stories her mother had shared to remind her of her childhood before they left New Zealand.

    By the last bite of scone, the last sip of tea, Lucy has tired of the past. The future seems infinitely more pressing. She can see a row of dress shops on the other side of the road. She wants something pretty, yet casual. But not too casual.

Chapter Seven

Ethan powers up the steps, cricket bag in one hand, helmet under the other arm, a white plastic grocery bag hanging in his other hand. He's hot and sweaty from an impromptu cricket practice, and not at all regretting his refusal to stick around for a beer afterwards.

He unlocks the door, dumping his gear on the kitchen floor, and checks his phone one more time. He is a bit pissed off that Georgie hasn't returned his texts, and decides it's nothing to do with the idiot she's doing; he's not about to tell her who she can and can't screw. At least he'll have the flat to himself tonight. He plugs his phone into its charger on the kitchen shelf then heads to the bedroom.

Ethan kicks his sneakers into the wardrobe, strips off his cricket whites and dumps them in the washing basket. He stands beside the bed for a moment, his hair damp with sweat, one hand rubbing over the erection growing beneath his boxer shorts. He slides his hand under the waistband and gives it a tug. A quick rub.

"Sheets!" he declares, purposefully passing up a quick wank, in favour of future possibilities. He struggles with a clean fitted sheet, and throws the duvet back on the bed. He balls up the old sheet and pushes it into the clothes basket.

Back in the kitchen, Ethan stands with the fridge door open and shrinks from its cool contents.

He pulls the rubbish bin over and proceeds to throw out anything green that really isn't supposed to be. Once a space is cleared, he takes out his newly purchased supplies and stacks them neatly on top of each other. Hummus, couscous salad and a flat tray of salmon kebabs resting on top, which he'll stick on the barbecue later.

He's gone with the fancy Kapiti ice cream for dessert. But he couldn't decide between the white chocolate and raspberry coulis, or the lemon meringue, so he's bought both. There's a slight ruckus as the iced-up freezer threatens to topple its contents out on to the floor, but Ethan manages to wedge the ice cream behind the fish fingers and close the door.

He once-overs the living room and doesn't think it's too bad. He stacks a pile of magazines, retrieves a couple of coffee mugs. He pulls the vacuum out from the hall cupboard and goes quickly over the places he can see crumbs.

Ethan showers quickly, giving himself directions.

"Check the barbecue has gas, set the table and put the wine in the fridge!"

Condoms. Just in case, Ethan thinks.

"Don't count your chickens," he tells the shower gel, before squeezing out a blob and rubbing it under both arms.

"Shit!"

He runs dripping to the kitchen, throws open the freezer door. He ignores the half-dozen fish fingers that fall to the floor as he digs into the supermarket bag. There, between the tubs of ice cream, is a three-pack of condoms.

Ethan had contemplated his options in the supermarket aisle while pretending he was perusing the shaving cream. *A drawer full of loose condoms might make me look like a bit of a player*, he thought, *yet a brand new box of twelve might be a little overwhelming, like I'd been planning on getting laid. A lot.*

"I'm more a quality over quantity bloke," he'd murmured to the shaving cream with extra aloe vera that he'd put in his basket, even though he had an electric shaver. He'd settled on the three-pack.

Three seems manageable, Ethan thinks, as he throws fish fingers back into the freezer and shoves the door closed. *Neither over-excited nor under-prepared.* He drips into the bedroom and puts them safely away in the drawer of his bedside table, then returns to the shower to rinse off.

Chapter Eight

Ethan smiles when Lucy appears at the gate, her cheeks flushed from the climb up the steps. He leaves his barbecue and welcomes Lucy to his house on the hill with a kiss on the cheek.

"I know you said not to bring anything," Lucy says, handing over an extra-large box of Roses chocolates, "but a little girl in the supermarket told me they were the bestest-ever in the whole world."

"They most definitely are," Ethan agrees, showing Lucy into the kitchen.

"Drink?" he asks, diving into the fridge, "I've got white wine or beer, or some kind of soda that's probably fizz-less." He holds up a half-full bottle of soda to illustrate.

"Wine is fine," Lucy smiles. She spies the pile of shoes at the door, and wonders if she should have removed hers, but Ethan is still in his flip-flops.

Should I sit? Should I wander around? Should I feign a headache and just go home? But I have no real home, just a bed in a hostel – and do I really want to hide out under my duvet?

Ethan solves her dilemma, handing her a cool glass of wine and insisting she look around while he "has a fiddle with the barbie."

"Georgie's room is on the left, mine's on the right, bathroom and loo in the middle," he calls from outside. The view from the window in the lounge is beautiful. Their lofty spot on the hill provides a clear view across the roofs of their neighbours and out to sea. The blue of the ocean is broken at times by little brown rock pools, but Lucy's eyes are pulled out into the distance, where a shadow of land seems to hang above the water.

"Kaikoura." Ethan says, coming and standing beside her. His beer bottle sits snugly in both his hands as he rocks from his toes to his heels and back again. "Right out there, in the distance. Kaikoura. The South Island," he explains. "Islands in the sun," Ethan sings, swapping words for whistling as he heads back out to the barbecue.

Lucy thinks dinner was delicious. She loves the little house on the hill and has perused the book collection, relieved to find a great number of popular fictions she has read, as well as a number of books about buildings and architecture, and a row of pocket travel guides.

"Have you been to Dubai?" she calls out.

"Not yet. Yourself?" Ethan calls back. Ethan thinks dinner went well, even though he forgot to take the couscous out of its plastic tub, and the salmon was a little over-cooked. He's searching for the fancy coffee, but it's nowhere to be found. "Instant okay?"

"Course," Lucy replies, "yes, once I went to Dubai," she gently eases into a demi plié. "A week of *Swan Lake*."

"More?" Ethan asks over the coffee mugs, so she finds fourth position and pirouettes, then ends with a curtsey. Ethan puts the coffee mugs on the bench and claps heartily.

"Ah, go on," Lucy laughs, and straightens the books on the shelf. "It's big."

"What is?"

"Dubai. It's massive. They drive fast. The hotels are fabulous."

"So I've heard," Ethan says, before he disappears in to the freezer. He retrieves the ice cream from behind the fish fingers.

"I always have my coffee with my ice cream," Ethan says.

With a spoon and a bowl each, they sit together on the couch, crunching the biscuity bits in the lemon meringue and sucking sweet white chocolate with tart raspberry swirl.

"All those buildings," Lucy says, licking the last of the ice cream from her spoon and using it to point to the collection of square canvas blocks that fill a small corner of wall beside the television. "Do you have a favourite? I've seen the Eiffel Tower, and the White House. I'd love to see the Great Wall of China. What's that bridge?" she asks.

"The Storbaelt. It's a suspension bridge that links the two main islands in Denmark. Funen and Zealand. Took about ten years to build. Cost about twenty-one billion dollars," he explains, taking both their bowls and carrying them to the kitchen. "It's actually two bridges and a tunnel." Lucy follows with the coffee mugs and watches as he fills the dishwasher. She wants to look at his face, but every time she does, her heart trips over itself and she can't breathe. So she turns way, instead concentrating on the picture of the bridge on the wall.

"It's huge," she says. Ethan closes the dishwasher, and moves to stand beside her. Her smooth bare legs below her sundress lined up next to his hairy legs below his shorts. They are close, side by side, leaning on the kitchen bench, looking through to the lounge. Ethan feels a first kiss is imminent, but she won't turn to face him.

"Eighteen kilometres long, and see that island in the middle," he says, "it's Sprogo. Between 1923 and 1956 they kept unmarried mothers and unstable women there."

"No way," Lucy laughs.

"The pathologically promiscuous, that's what they called them. At the time they thought it was great," he explains, "it meant they didn't have to lock them up in jail."

"But taking them away from their families and dumping them on an island?" Lucy tells Ethan that there is a high likelihood she and her mother would have ended up on Sprogo. "My mother and father never married, she's never really said why, only that it was never meant to be."

"How old were you," Ethan asks, "when you left?"

"I was six." Lucy scratches an itch on her elbow, "I don't remember being sad about it," she says. "I had a room at Gran and Granddad's with a real dollhouse that used to be my mum's. The floorboards squeaked, and my gran had a dachshund called Gavin." Lucy smiles, and Ethan likes how her face lights up. "I haven't thought of him in years. I remember how much fun it was to make him yap, with everyone then telling him to shush."

Ethan listens happily to Lucy's memories of sitting in the

garden eating strawberries dusted in icing sugar. "Gran picked horses from the paper and their names always made me giggle. Cheerful Cherry, Fun in the Sun..."

"Martini Henri!" Ethan says.

Lucy laughs, "Like the drink?" she asks.

"No it's actually a type of gun. First New Zealand horse to win the Melbourne Cup. An Australian race – it's a really big thing here. Anyway, it doesn't sound like your gran would have shipped your mum off to an island for unwed mothers," Ethan muses.

"I suppose not," Lucy smiles.

Ethan and Lucy stand side by side. *God, I want to kiss her,* Ethan thinks. Lucy scrapes together as much boldness as she can find and turns to look at his face.

"Hello," he says, and his eyes crinkle at the edges when he smiles. There is a rough shadow of whiskers forming on his chin line that Lucy longs to reach out and run her hand along, but he's beaten her to it.

"Pixie Shooting Butts." Ethan says. "First pet and the name of the first street I lived on. "That's what I'd call my racehorse."

"Your first pet was called Pixie, and you lived on a street called Shooting Butts?" Lucy stands with her hands on her hips and raises her eyebrows.

"Pixie was a small Angora goat who liked to chew on my T-shirts," Ethan tells Lucy, "and no, not a street called Shooting Butts. A road. And I can prove it."

Ethan takes his mobile phone from the counter and slides

in behind Lucy. She can feel his chest rise and fall at her back while he taps on his phone and waits for the map to appear. His head rests lightly on top of her own as he scrolls the screen to the right place. "See!" he says, pointing to the pin on the screen and enclosing her in his arms as he does so. Ethan feels her lean into him, hears the slight wobble in her voice as she exclaims, "Bloody hell, it's true! I bet no one ever believes you!"

He puts the phone back on the bench and turns her around to look at him. There is no space left between them. He slides his hand into hers and walks himself backwards a couple of paces, pulling Lucy forwards, so that he can lean against the countertop without letting her go. His legs are slightly parted, leaving just enough room for hers in between them. His thighs feel strong. Ethan loops a hand around her waist, gently bringing her in. *I should just bloody well kiss him,* Lucy thinks, but she feels shy, and nervous, and inexplicably on the brink of something more important than the shallow breaths she is only just able to take.

The slow and steady build-up of tension is as pleasurable for Ethan as if had he lifted her skirt and taken her on the kitchen counter, with all the lust his body is channelling. But Ethan doesn't want a quickie. He doesn't want a wham bam; he wants much more than that this evening, thank you ma'am! He wants to watch her. Lucy's eyes are locked on his chin and she won't make eye contact. Her shyness is both enchanting and challenging.

"Your turn," he says, rocking her gently towards him as

both a prompt, and a chance to bump his growing erection against her hip.

Lucy feels a rush of heat, every sense is strung tight. She can smell him. She wants to feel him and taste him and her body is buzzing in anticipation.

"Your first pet and your first street name," Ethan prompts, again rocking her forward but this time holding her close. Her hips press against his. Her cheeks flush and her nipples grow visible through the thin cotton of her dress.

"God, um, my first pet was a cat called Winston. And though I'd have to confirm it, I think we lived on Peters Ave. Or was it Peters Terrace?" She's not sure and she can't think straight anyway.

Just kiss me Ethan, damn it.

Ethan whistles low and long. "A racehorse called Winston Peters. You know he's a politician here? Bit of a legend. Reputation for being quite unruly."

"What did he do?" Lucy asks.

"I can't really remember – something to do with a box of wine?" Ethan suggests.

"Anyway," Lucy says, "I don't think that is the way you name a racehorse. Isn't it how you find your porn star name?"

"Possibly," Ethan agrees, "are you in the market for a porn star name?" But before she can respond, he finds the corner of her mouth with his own. He works his lips over hers and his tongue into her mouth. His hips grind against her and Lucy can't remember what they were talking about and she doesn't care. She keeps her eyes closed and lets the sensation of his kisses wash over her. His mouth is warm and firm and she has little control over the small gasp and sigh that escapes as he slips one hand under her dress, and his fingers rub against her soft lace knickers.

Ethan is enchanted. He's bewitched by a girl in a cotton sundress who has no knowledge of her powers. Her arms are around his neck; her hands gripping his hair at the base of his neck. Her lips are glued to his and every now and then they break apart to gasp for air before diving back together. He lets his hand cup her breast, his fingers flick gently over her nipples, and imagines what they will be like to lick and suck.

Lucy can't remember ever feeling so horny. She lets her fingers travel the length of his spine and moves a leg over his so that she can straddle his thigh. He mumbles "Holy hell," and Lucy smiles through his kisses.

They have no sense of time or place, until Ethan's phone jumps to life, vibrating on the countertop between shrill beeps.

"Fuck," Ethan smiles, kissing her again.

"It's got dark outside," Lucy laughs.

He keeps one arm around Lucy's waist, unwilling to let her go, and reaches for the phone with the express purpose of pressing END CALL, sending the inconsiderate caller to his mail box. But it stops before he can. The screen glows green between them.

"It was just Georgie," he says. His finger is on the power off button when the phone alights again, buzzing and beeping.

"Answer it," Lucy says, "I'll just use your bathroom."

He reluctantly lets her out of his embrace, and sighs as he moves his finger to the green button.

"This better be good," he growls, "'cause your timing is shit!" Ethan hears a whimper, a loud hiccupping sob.

"Georgie?" he says loudly into the phone, "is that you?"

"Yes," a hiccupping sob takes over again, "co-co-co-come and get me."

Lucy hears the panic in Ethan's voice before she's left the bathroom.

"Where are you?" he's yelling. "Just stay there, don't move. I'm on my way."

"Georgie needs a ride," is all he will tell Lucy. The flick of a switch fills the kitchen with a harsh white light that exposes the panic in Ethan's eyes, mirroring his voice. "Can you grab my wallet and keys from beside my bed?" Ethan ducks into Georgie's room, returning with a polar fleece jersey and a pair of track pants. Lucy holds out the wallet and keys. "Come on," he urges, and shuffles her out the door.

Lucy is cautious on the steps, willing her eyes to adjust to the sudden changes in light. Ethan fusses behind her, knowing he would usually skip them two or three at a time but trying to be patient.

"God, woman," he says, exasperated, and lifts her off her feet, carrying her down the last ten steps.

Chapter Nine

"Bad news. *Knew* that bloke was bad news." His words are clipped. At the traffic lights he holds her hand briefly. Lucy holds in her lap his worn leather wallet, stuffed with receipts and business cards. We'll take the cutting," he says, and the car snakes up and over a tall windy hill. The lights of the houses twinkle below them as they dip back down to sea level.

"I should have warned her. Have before, but she doesn't really listen. Stubborn arse."

Lucy rubs her finger along the frayed seam of his wallet and nods. She would like to say something reassuring, but she's only met Georgie the once. And she's a bit worried her presence might not be very welcome. Lucy can't help wondering if Ethan and Georgie have history. She thinks she might be in the middle of something.

Why didn't I wait at the house? Or get a taxi home?

"If she's got hypothermia, I'm dumping her outside the hospital." Lucy knows that isn't true.

"No you won't." she says.

"No. I won't." Ethan sighs.

They turn right, Ethan driving a little faster than the speed limit, then suddenly stopping to U-turn in front of a small wooden building.

"Balaena Bay," Lucy reads the sign on what looks like a

small boat house. Ethan leans over her and digs around in the glove box. He switches a small silver torch on and off, then slams the glove box door shut.

"Wait here," he demands, and then he is gone.

She can hear his crunching footsteps, then he disappears down below the line of the road, and all that is left is the soft swish of the water lapping at the shore she cannot see. Lucy presses her face up to the car window in the hopes of making out a human figure in the darkness, but the moon is lost behind a bank of clouds and the shadows are still.

She turns her attention from the sea below, to the hill that rises, cliff-like, on the other side of the road. She wonders how the houses perched above her stay moored to their foundations. She is mesmerised by a small cottage tucked in to the base of the cliff, its front window glowing under the weight of hundreds of tiny twinkle lights. She imagines the occupants beyond the window. *Do the lights stay on all night? Or has someone forgotten to flick the switch off,* she ponders, *as they usually would on the way to bed? Are they sitting there, on the other side of the black glass, sipping cups of coffee and watching me, sitting here, watching them?* Lucy shivers. She leans over the driver's side and is reassured by the loud click of the central locking.

It's a long ten minutes before she hears footsteps and voices, and sees the light from the torch guiding the way.

"Fuck off, then," Georgie is slurring, her voice scratchy and confused.

"I was just saying," Ethan is scrambling to catch up with

her, "that you could have got yourself, you know, killed or something."

"God, you're dramatic," Georgie says, stumbling against the bonnet of the car. Lucy opens the passenger door and stands beside it, unsure what to do.

Georgie is scantily clad, in just a bra and knickers; the soft curve of her stomach wobbles as she stumbles in a sort of circle. Georgie obviously needs their help, yet she is brazen and bullish. Her hair is matted and contains what looks like bits of branch and sand.

"What's she doing here?" Georgie asks, hands on hips and chest jutting out so that her left nipple rises above the edge of her bra with every breath. She takes a step closer to Lucy. "Do I *know* you?" Georgie asks, closing one eye tightly and glaring with the other.

"For fuck's sake," Ethan yells, "she's with me. She came with me."

"I carried a watermelon." Lucy says quietly.

"What?" Georgie asks.

"I carried a watermelon," Lucy says again, a little louder.

Ethan scrunches his nose up in confusion, but Georgie is smiling.

"She carried a watermelon," she cries, "she carried a bloody watermelon." She slaps the pale white skin of her thigh and heaves in drunken laughter. "She carried a watermelon." Georgie is hiccupping and laughing. Lucy laughs too.

"It's from *Dirty Dancing*," she tells Ethan.

"The power of alcohol." he sighs.

"She carried a fucking watermelon, but did you bring Patrick Swayze?" Georgie asks, and she's off again, laughing and swaying, until her legs give way and she is on her hands and knees. And then her laughter turns to sobs. Gut wrenching, heart-felt sobs that come from deep within. There are half-heard words that make no sense in the slur and stutter of Georgie's lowest of lows. The brazen and bullish is replaced with a rawness of emotion that, for too many seconds, leaves Lucy and Ethan frozen before her, their sober minds slower to accept the change in sensibility.

"Blimey," Ethan says, but it is Lucy who moves. She sits down on the grass and dirt, and envelopes Georgie in a hug, because she knows that is what she would want someone to do for her. She tells Ethan to get Georgie some clothes, and she pats her tangled hair and says, "shhh," and "there, there," and waits for her sobs to decrease in volume. Lucy lets them fade into whispered whimpers, then she and Ethan put Georgie in the back seat of the car and take her home.

Georgie is sick once, halfway up the eighty-two steps. Lucy sends Ethan on ahead to warm up the shower then, when Georgie is able, the two girls finish the climb. The chirp of a single cicada and a thousand slurred sorries carry them up, one step at a time, to the little house on the hill.

Georgie stands motionless in the shower, her bra and knickers still on. Lucy doesn't feel she knows her well enough to take on that challenge.

"I'm sorry," is all she says. Ethan has disappeared, making

noises about boiling water and warming towels.

"She's not having a baby," Lucy giggles to herself while she uses the spray nozzle to rinse Georgie's hair.

"I'm not a baby," Georgie whispers, then closes her eyes, "I'm sorry," she says again, and Lucy returns to her hush-hush noises.

The branches in Georgie's hair turned out to be bits of seaweed, which Lucy leaves in a little pile on the window sill, rather than letting them wash down and block the drain. She blobs an overly generous amount of shampoo on to Georgie's head and does her best to massage it in. A thin line of sand coats the bottom of the shower as the soap is rinsed from Georgie's hair. Ethan hovers by the door with two towels and a blue nightie.

"I can do it now," Georgie whispers, "I think I can do it now."

They busy themselves in the kitchen. Ethan spoons Milo into mugs and Lucy finds the milk in the fridge. When she appears from the bathroom, Georgie is pale, but she is more stable on her feet, which she uses to carry her to the corner of the couch, then tucks them away under the ball she has rolled her body into.

"Cold?" Lucy asks. "Blanket?"

"Duvet?" Georgie asks, accepting the mug of Milo that Ethan is holding out to her. Lucy retrieves the quilt from Georgie's bed and settles into the other side of the couch.

"Toast." Ethan calls from the kitchen, "Marmite? Vegemite?"

"What's Vegemite?" Lucy asks Georgie, who makes

vomiting motions and assures her, "It's disgusting."

"Marmite times two," Lucy calls back to the kitchen.

"Your loss," Ethan shrugs, warming his hands over the toaster as he waits for the pop.

"I'm so sorry," Georgie says again, "I'm so embarrassed. I'm totally not usually like this, I promise." Lucy nods and sips her Milo, noting the slur in Georgie's voice is beginning to ease.

"That's a lie," Georgie admits. "I'm totally like this. I mean I don't usually end up naked on the roadside. That was a first." She seems to drift off somewhere else, staring at a spot on the carpet that offers no clue to her inner thoughts.

"This is going to sound so stupid. Even in my head I know how stupid I was, but I just thought if I tried hard enough, if I was cool enough or sexy enough, or daring enough, that he'd see how great we were, how things could work out." A single tear trickles gently down Georgie's cheek, and Lucy shuffles a little closer on the couch, tucking her own feet under the duvet.

"Men, eh?" she whispers, for she is struggling to find the right words for the situation, when she doesn't know Georgie that well and is still at a loss as to what exactly has happened.

"It's my fault, really. I dared him. We were on the night bus and I dared him. 'I dare you to go skinny dipping with me.' That's what I said. He thought I was a bit mad, but I goaded him. I called him a chicken. I said 'Come on, mummy's boy.' So we got off the bus. He didn't wait for me – left me to scramble down the bank to the stony beach alone. Then and there, I knew he just wanted to pass the challenge. It had nothing to do with me. He was stripped down to his boxers and in the water before I'd pulled my dress off."

Lucy watches Georgie pause again, the same spot on the carpet holding her attention. The smell of toast wafts into the lounge, making Lucy's stomach rumble. It's hours since the couscous and salad that she had been too nervous to eat very much of.

Georgie's next words pour out in a torrent. She'd called into the darkness and followed his voice into the sea, where they'd laughed and shivered in the cool water.

"You're a daft tart," he'd said, and in the darkness Georgie had taken it as a compliment.

"But that's why you love me," she'd replied, wrapping her arms around his cool stomach and willing him to mirror her actions.

"Who says I love you?" was what he said instead, the edge of humour gone from his voice. But Georgie had been too pissed to pick up on the subtle change, and had shimmied around him, sing-songing into the shallow bay, "You love me, you love me."

"That's when he pushed me. We were only thigh deep in water," Georgie quickly justifies, seeing the look of horror cross Lucy's face.

"Fuck off," he'd said, and stormed up to the beach, with Georgie scrambling to catch up.

"I was only teasing," she tried to tell him, as he fought to get his wet legs into his jeans, "chill out." But he'd got right up in her face, so close she could smell the faint whiff of cigarettes mixed with the salty water still moist on his skin.

"This has nothing to do with love. I told you at the start, I don't need that crap. I like you, you're a good shag. But this is not love." Georgie told him to calm down, that she hadn't meant anything by it, but he'd stalked off, leaving her alone on the beach, shuffling and shivering in the darkness, looking for her belongings.

She had waited a few minutes, sure he'd return. But he didn't. She had fished her phone out of her bag and called. It went to message twice before he answered.

'Whatever you thought this was, it's over,' he had told her. 'It was fun but, you know, time to move on.' There was half of a small hip-flask of gin in her handbag, so Georgie had sat on the beach and finished it.

"I felt numb – I wanted to feel numb. But then I got scared. So I rang Ethan."

Ethan polishes his toast off in a series of big bites. He watches Lucy munch thoughtfully while Georgie nibbles hers like a little mouse, managing one small triangle before abandoning the plate on the side of the couch.

"Maybe I should call him," she says, "maybe he just needed a chance to cool off."

"I'm no expert," Lucy says, "but two a.m. phone calls are rarely, if ever, a good idea."

The night slides effortlessly into the wee hours of the morning, and the two girls talk on, filling the lulls with information about each other.

"I didn't go to normal school," Lucy explains, "I studied between ballet classes. I still managed to get my A levels."

"I was a nerdy swat," Georgie explains, "then in sixth form I discovered boys, and it all went to hell."

"I once kept a tally of how many cans of hairspray I was using in a year. I stopped counting at seventy-two."

"I love my job," Georgie says, and Lucy can tell she means it. Her eyes are animated for the first time. "I mean it's nothing important really. Social media, I tweet a lot, and share celebrity gossip. I give a lot of stuff away. I get to go to the Rugby Sevens each year."

"I'm a has-been dancer, looking for something to be."

"I need to go to bed," Ethan yawns.

"You can sleep on the couch," Georgie assures Lucy, since it's now edging two in the morning. "I'll lend you a T-shirt."

Ethan goes to brush his teeth. He's pissed off at Georgie. She's stolen his night, his plans. He was so close, but the pack of condoms will remain unopened in the drawer beside his bed.

"May as well have left them in the freezer," he grumbles.

He wants to return and say good night – he intends on giving Georgie a look that will say 'bugger off,' but from the hallway he can hear her muffled sobs.

"Maybe it wasn't as bad as I thought," he hears her say. "Maybe I just pushed too hard, too fast. Maybe he's cooled down." And he hears Lucy, saying that even though she does not know Georgie that well at all, and Georgie doesn't have to listen to her advice at all – because god knows she is not very good at taking her own advice at the best of times – but she thinks Georgie should remember that Felix left her alone on a beach, in the middle of the night. That he hadn't come back for her, or called to check she was okay. And that even from the little time she had sat here with Georgie, Lucy insisted that she knew Georgie was worth more than that. Didn't Georgie think she deserved better?

"I guess so," Georgie agreed, the sobs coming thick and fast now, "I just don't know what I did wrong."

Ethan decides to leave them alone. He pulls up the duvet and decides that he can wait. He has a meeting at eight-thirty, and he should go in early and prep. *Or maybe I'll just wing it,* he thinks. Though this is an important meeting, Dubai hasn't exactly been at the forefront of Ethan's mind this week. And though sleep comes easily, Ethan spends the night racing on the back of a camel, whose big lips blow raspberries at him every time he crosses the finish line last.

Chapter Ten

Lucy saw Georgie off to bed around three-thirty in the morning, and has slept, dreamless, curled in a small ball in the corner of what turned out to be a very comfortable couch. Ethan's sleeping bag has kept her snug and warm, and though she has sniffed and inhaled deeply to see if the slightest scent of him might have remained squashed into the bag along with the feathers, there is nothing there.

It is the sound of the electric kettle whistling that stirs Lucy awake, and she wriggles round so that one sleepy eye can spy who is in the kitchen. *I spy with my little eye, someone beginning with E.* It is the first time Lucy has seen him in anything other than shorts and shirts. His trousers are a light grey and his shoes are shiny black. His shirt is white and when he turns to get the milk from the fridge, she sees a pale blue tie dangling loosely from his unbuttoned collar. He is whistling, which Lucy is trying to ignore. *Whistling only ever sounds good to the person who is doing the whistling,* she thinks. But he carries on, oblivious. She watches him dunk two tea bags on strings in and out of two mugs, his foot tapping in time to his whistling, and Lucy thinks maybe, just maybe, she could live with the whistling.

"You're awake!" he smiles, setting a mug of tea down on the coffee table in front of her and moving to the window where he sips from his own and contemplates the day ahead.

"Clouds are looking a bit grey out there," he notes, as Lucy sits up, cross-legged in the sleeping bag, and takes small sips of tea, blowing steam from the top of the mug and trying to smooth her hair, which she can feel is a tangle of curls and knots.

"I've got a meeting at eight-thirty," Ethan says, coming to sit beside Lucy on the couch. "Nothing exciting," he continues, then wonders why he feels the need to qualify the information and, furthermore, why he has done so with a lie. A job on the other side of the world, helping project-manage the build of large skyscrapers, is nothing if not exciting, not to mention what he has been working so hard for over the last eight years.

They talk briefly about Georgie, skirting over the basics: that she is going to go home to her mum's for the weekend, and yes, they agree, she'll be okay, she'll bounce back. Georgie is one of his best friends, Ethan explains to Lucy. She always goes for losers like Felix and he just wants her to find someone who can see that she is funny and kind and worth getting to know.

And here is Lucy, he thinks, as he absent-mindedly loops his own pinkie finger with hers, squeezing gently. Even in the few hours spent together the previous evening, Ethan knows he is hooked. He likes the small pauses she takes before she offers her opinions, the way she looks up at the ceiling when she is trying to find the right words.

"Shall I meet you back here at five-thirty?" he asks.

"Dinner? Out? Somewhere? There's a Thai place? Round the

corner? If you want to?" Ethan speaks every word as a question.

"Okay," Lucy says, suddenly very busy running her finger over the scratchy metal zip of the sleeping bag.

"Okay," Ethan says, and because he hasn't brushed his teeth yet, he offers her a chaste kiss on the hand, and goes to sort himself out.

Lucy sips her tea and watches him potter. He has a lunchbox, and Lucy smiles when he tips a pile of last night's leftovers on to one slice of bread and squishes another slice on top. She likes the way his nose crinkles up as he contemplates how he's going to get the giant sandwich into its container, and she hides her laughter under the sleeping bag when he uses a fish slice and yells "ta-da!" when the sandwich is suitably secured.

Ethan disappears into his bedroom and returns with a helmet and a backpack. His tie now sits snugly below his Adam's apple; a brown leather jacket hangs over his arm.

"I'll see you at five-thirty," he says. "Help yourself in the kitchen if you're hungry – I left a towel for you beside the bathroom sink."

"Have a lovely day at work," Lucy says. *I'd quite like to see him to the door,* she thinks, *maybe a kiss goodbye on the step there,* she ponders. But she's only wearing her knickers and an old T-shirt of Georgie's, and climbing out of the sleeping bag with him watching her is not something she's game for. *I could blow him a kiss,* she thinks, moving her arm to do so, but the naffness of it isn't lost on Lucy and she quickly turns it into a small, slightly odd wave.

Ethan would like to dive on top of her. Crawl inside his sleeping bag with her and not come out till lunchtime. Dinnertime, maybe! But he's already running late, so he grabs a banana, tucks his helmet under his arm and sends her a wink on the way out the door. *Did I just wink at her? Bloody hell.*

Lucy listens to him whistling down the stairs, to the sound of the garage door rumbling up and his scooter spluttering to life. When silence returns, it is not uncomfortable. Lucy tiptoes to the loo, then to the kitchen, where she peels a banana. She sees that the time on the microwave clock reads only 7.38am. She quickly counts on her fingers: *4, 5, 6, 7am... four hours' sleep. Madness!* She climbs back into Ethan's sleeping bag. She finishes the banana, leaving the skin draped over the edge of her empty tea mug, and snuggles back down into the squashy cushions.

Whistling. Bloody hell, someone else is whistling now, Lucy thinks as she blinks her eyes awake. But no one is there, and it takes a moment for her to realise that with each blustery gust of wind, a small gap in the window lets a small breeze into the room, whistling its presence. There is a bag of rubbish tied up by the front door and a small overnight bag sits open in the middle of the kitchen floor.

"You're up!" Georgie smiles, dumping a toilet bag and a well-thumbed book into the bag and zipping it up. "It's only nine-fifteen," Georgie hurries to add, "no need to be embarrassed," watching Lucy sit up quickly and try to fight a yawn. "I'm one of those terrible early morning people," Georgie explains. "Coffee?"

"Yes, please," Lucy says.

"Even after last night, I was awake at eight this morning. You looked zonked so I went for a run. Well, more of a brisk walk. I nearly threw up on Medway Street." Georgie pushes her Ipod into the speaker cradle on the bench and the radio springs to life. "I love this song," she says, "Makes me a total cougar, I know. It's probably illegal; I think one of them is fifteen." Georgie sets about banging plates and mugs, opening and closing the fridge door and filling the jug with water. "I got us some breakfast," she says, "and then I sorted out the rubbish because it's My. Job." Lucy can hear the capital letters in Georgie's words. "Ethan does the washing," she elaborates. "I do the rubbish. He whines like a child about having to separate the recycling. Then I had a shower, and now you're up! Sugar?"

"Two, please," Lucy sits up straighter and watches Georgie move about her kitchen, wondering if this girl can be the same one who has been bending over backwards to make a total knob like that Felix fall in love with her.

"You probably think I'm nuts," Georgie says, putting the fresh mug of coffee down and taking the old mugs from Ethan and Lucy's early morning tea for two. She returns with her own mug of coffee and a plate of fresh blueberry muffins. "They're from the café on the parade," she says, "the one next to the dry cleaners. Not the one next to the fish and chip shop. They use packet mix." Georgie peels the muffin paper back, dropping a pile of crumbs on the carpet in the process. "You have to try their carrot cake with the cream cheese icing – divine." Lucy takes a muffin and listens happily as Georgie flits from one topic to the next. She almost rang Felix. She wants to, "...but at the same time, it just feels wrong. I want to believe I'm worth more than that."

"You are," Lucy assures her, "you're too lovely for him," and though she has known Georgie for less than a day, she can see that Ethan is right; this vivacious and funny woman needs someone better. Deserves someone lovely. She tries to tell Georgie as much and is rewarded with an elbow in the side and another muffin.

A knock at the door surprised both girls.

"Bloody hell, you're early," Georgie yells at the front door.

"Shall I piss off without you, then?" a man's voice calls back.

Georgie trails crumbs through the lounge and kitchen. She unbolts the front door and walks away, back to her seat beside Lucy on the couch. The man seems unperturbed. He dumps his keys on the counter and pours coffee from the plunger into a mug.

"The hostess with the mostest, Gee-Gee," he says, taking a muffin from the plate on the coffee table.

"That was the last one," Georgie protests, "you pig."

"You snooze, you lose. I'm Chris," he says, holding his hand out over the coffee table to Lucy. "You're from London, yeah?"

"I told him about you this morning," Georgie explains,

"Chris is an old friend from university. He has a very nice car and he's going to drive me over the hill to Masterton."

Chris flicks crumbs from his muffin at her. "I was her university saviour," Chris tells Lucy, "her Economics tutor. She'd have failed without me. I do have a nice car, it's a Mazda RX8."

"It's red," Georgie says, "and it's got a sunroof."

"Lovely!" Lucy says.

She watches them scrap over who is going to carry the bag down the stairs. Georgie wins that one, and Lucy waves goodbye to them both from the safety of her sleeping bag on the couch. She listens to them bickering about whether they're going to stop at McDonald's for lunch, who's paying the petrol and who gets to listen to which CD first until their voices turn to mumbles and she hears car doors open and shut. *Now those two would make a good couple.*

Lucy rolls up the sleeping bag and tucks it away in the cupboard, where she finds a small vacuum cleaner that does a good job of sucking up the muffin crumbs. She showers quickly, not being sure how long the hot water will last. She uses the conditioner on the shelf that smells like apples, the large blue towel Ethan has left out for her, and borrows Georgie's hair dryer. Looking in the mirror, even though she is back in yesterday's sun-dress, Lucy feels, and feels like she looks, much better. She retrieves her tote bag from beside the couch, slips on a fresh pair of knickers and takes her toothbrush to the bathroom, where she spends extra time staring at herself in the mirror and smiling through the frothy toothpaste.

She empties the dishwasher next, making a little row on the counter of bowls and cups she can't find homes for.

I am in Ethan's house.

I am emptying Ethan's dishwasher.

I am looking out the window of Ethan's house.

There is nothing left for Lucy to do but wait for Ethan, and though she knows he will be worth the wait, watching the minutes tick by on the microwave clock is making her nervous. She decides on a quick trip back to the hostel for a change of clothes. The storm clouds beyond the window are brewing and her sundress and cardigan aren't offering much warmth. But, having checked her wallet and found only a fifty dollar note, and knowing full well that bus drivers in any location do not take kindly to such large denominations, Lucy is on a hunt for bus money.

There is no money jar in the kitchen, no loose change in the kitchen drawer. She pads quietly to Ethan's bedroom and hovers by the door. White sheets, pale green duvet. Two normal-sized pillows with matching green slips. Yesterday's flip flops peeking out from under the bed.

She tiptoes into the room and slides Ethan's bedside drawer open. She finds a pile of dollar coins, and a box of unopened condoms.

He's waiting, too.

Chapter Eleven

Ethan's scooter carries him around the Basin Reserve and up Adelaide Road, down into Island Bay. Home to his house on the hill, home to Lucy who is waiting at the window.

Lucy's bus back to the little house on the hill arrived about an hour ago, and she's been reluctant to leave the window ever since. At the hostel, she paid up for another three nights. She has changed into her jeans, a light pink shirt and a soft grey cardigan. Her tote bag holds a spare T-shirt and knickers, just in case she might stay the night again. And her tangle-free conditioning spray. And her toothbrush. *Just in case.*

When his scooter appears around the corner, Lucy is unsure what to do. She jumps back from the window, and is overcome by a giggling snort. She clamps a hand over her mouth and holds her breath. She can hear the garage door closing, knows he'll be climbing the stairs. *Should I put the telly on? But I've no idea what remote to use. He'll think I've just been sitting here waiting for him.*

Well, haven't I? Isn't that exactly what I've been doing? I don't want him to think I'm over-eager. I don't want to scare him off. Lucy throws herself on the couch and grabs a magazine, some kind of television guide. *They have Coro here,* she tells herself over her beating heart and the rush of blood to her ears when she hears a key in the door. *But only on a*

Thursday and a Friday.

Ethan takes his time on the stairs, and tries to plan the evening. *Cup of coffee and then out for dinner? Early dinner then a walk along the beach? Will the rain hold off?*

He opens the door and Lucy is there, on the couch, reading last week's TV guide.

"Hey," he says, dumping his helmet on the counter and unzipping his jacket.

"Hey," she says, standing up, then not knowing whether to sit down again.

But there is no need to worry. She watches him shrug off his jacket and hang it on the back of a chair. He comes and stands in front of her, and once again his body is pressed against her own.

"Hey," he says again, then his mouth is on hers and in hers with an urgency that leaves her breathless. He walks her slowly backwards to his bedroom, undoing the buttons of her shirt on the way, his mouth refusing to leave her own.

Lucy can't form a single sensible thought about anything. She pulls his shirt free from his trousers and her hands travel the length of his spine, pressing him closer to her. His ragged breath matches her own and in a matter of seconds his tie is off, his shirt unbuttoned and in a pile on the floor with his trousers. Her own clothes are quick to follow. He turns her around and lets his hand whisper gently across her shoulder blades, then gently unclips her bra.

"And these?" He whispers kisses along her shoulder, then she feels his hands ease her knickers down, letting them fall to the floor. Lucy turns to face Ethan. His mouth joins hers once more and Lucy lets her hands roam, exploring new territory. The curve of his bum, the firmness of muscles, the whisper of his hair. She closes her eyes and waits while the drawer beside Ethan's bed slides open, and she smiles at the sound of the plastic wrap being wrestled from the outside of the box.

"Fuck," Ethan says. Lucy opens her eyes, and they both laugh nervously, while Ethan tries to steady his hand and slide on the condom.

"You're cold," Ethan says, running a hand over the goose bumps on her arm.

"Warm me up?" Lucy asks, and Ethan lies her down, covering her body with his own, his erection pressed firmly against her thigh. His hand finds the soft give of her breast, the hard point of her nipple. He holds it between his fingers and rolls gently. Lucy can't breathe. She can hear herself moan, feels his mouth sucking on her neck, then opens her eyes and watches his mouth cover her breast, feels his tongue circle and suck. Lucy closes her eyes again, sliding her hips till she feels the tip of his erection. She feels Ethan's back muscles tense as she rubs herself against him. Lucy feels the fizz of lust and laughter and longing, and wriggles underneath him.

"Bloody hell," he growls, making Lucy wriggle more.

It's about all Ethan can take. He slides inside Lucy, breathing deeply through that exquisite first thrust. Her head is thrown back, her eyes closed as she raises her hips to meet his. She finds a rhythm for them both, lets her mind and body empty, then welcomes the slow build-up of tension. Ethan gives in to the urge to push harder and deeper. Lucy wraps her legs around him, crying out as the intense waves of emotion wash over her, and as the last of Lucy's orgasm subsides, Ethan tips over the edge, and Lucy squeezes her pelvic muscles tightly. She is rewarded with a ragged "Holy fuck", as he throbs inside her.

Lucy lies on her side, her hand resting on Ethan's chest, feeling the rise and fall as his breath returns to normal.

"Raining," Lucy says, and they listen to the spits hit the roof and blow against the window.

"That was incredible," Ethan says. Lucy smiles, letting her fingers tiptoe along the length of his collarbone and back again. Ethan's fingers gently graze her lower back, sending pleasant shivers up and down her spine.

"You've got goose bumps again," he says, turning to face her and placing a warm hand on her cool shoulder. "Under the covers?" he asks, and a ruckus of blanket kicking and laughter ensues.

They meet once again, under the duvet, hips touching, legs entwined.

"It's a quilt." Lucy says. Their kisses are softer, their touch and taste less urgent.

"It's a duvet," Ethan responds, cupping her breast in his hand and gently flicking his thumb over her nipple. Lucy feels fantastic. She loves the length in Ethan's back, the soft damp curls at the back of his neck, the way his mouth wanders away, but always returns to kiss her mouth. She likes that he lingers.

I could compare, or contrast, or consider, Lucy thinks. *But thinking is distracting when, right now...* her body is entwined with Ethan's... *I'm just going to enjoy,* she decides. *I'm enjoying Ethan!*

And Ethan is enjoying Lucy. *Lovely, luscious, lusty! Lucy,* he thinks, as she pushes his hand away and slides down beneath the sheets.

Bloody hell, Lucy!

Ethan misses the faint buzz of his cell phone, buried as it is in his jacket hanging on the back of the dining room chair. But it is only Georgie, leaving a text message to say she's made it to Masterton, her mum says hi, and she'll be back on Monday night.

Say hi to Lucy for me she says, Go forth and shag her!

Ethan will get the message tomorrow and laugh at the timing.

Lucy's phone will also have a missed call, but the international number is not one she will recognise, and when she checks the message she will hear a man's muffled voice say,

"Damn," then hang up. She'll briefly consider the muffled man, and she will feel a bit odd for a moment. Something will squeeze in her chest and she will scrunch her toes into the carpet. She might say "shit". Or she might whisper "not fair". But Ethan will call to her to hurry up, that he is starving. He'll pinch her bum as he squeezes past her on the way to brush his teeth.

Lucy will decide it was probably a wrong number. And she will stuff her cell phone back in her bag. She will follow him into the bathroom, check her reflection in the mirror and wish she had thought to bring her turquoise beaded necklace.

Ethan will kiss the back of her neck, and go to find the car keys. Then he'll yell out that he's bloody well leaving without her, and Lucy will quickly slick on some lip gloss and she'll be gone.

Phone call forgotten.

Chapter Twelve

"He sounds bloody marvellous, but when was the last time you left the house?" Liz asks. The slight fuzz on the line and the delay in Lucy receiving her voice is frustrating.

"We've been getting to know each other," Lucy smiles, stretching her legs out in the sunshine.

"You mean you've been having sex," Liz corrects her best friend.

"Lots," Lucy giggles. "Anyway, you tart, I bet you're in bed, eating Minstrels and watching Stephen Fry." Liz feels happy to be chatting to her friend, but wishes she wasn't so far away.

"You're wrong," she says, "They're Maltesers and I'm on the couch, and Fry time isn't for another half an hour."

"We're going out today," Lucy says proudly, "Ethan is taking me on a picnic to a lighthouse. He's a project manager, did I tell you that?"

"In both email and text!" Liz confirms. "It's been snowing here – you'd never know spring was supposed to be just around the corner. *Cinderella* starts in two weeks, so rehearsals are ramping up."

"Oh you lucky thing," Lucy says, feeling a little jealous. A wave of homesickness washes over her as she imagines the warmth of her workmates arriving each morning in thick winter coats. The smell of coffee, the array of Starbucks and

Costa coffee cups littering the corners of their dressing rooms.

"I think I've got a job," Lucy tells Liz. "There's a ballet school down the road. It's next to the fish and chip shop and the junior teacher is pregnant. She's sick as a dog, all day – not just morning sickness, so I've a trial on Saturday morning with the little ones. The under-fives. It's just part time. Twenty-five hours a week."

"Good for you!" Liz cries. "You're brilliant with the sprogs."

"Put some sunblock on," Liz hears Ethan in the background, "burn time is only twelve minutes today."

"I hate you both," Liz says, "I think we had some sunshine last Tuesday for half an hour."

Liz leaves Lucy and Ethan to their picnic and takes herself off to bed for Fry time, but even Stephen's dulcet tones can't shake the slight concern she feels for her friend.

Even when Lucy was in the room next door, there were times when Liz could feel her disappear. She thinks back to the young girl who arrived at rehearsals for *Sleeping Beauty* with a wealth of determination and stamina that never faded. It didn't matter how long rehearsals dragged on, or how hard the director from hell pushed, hoping to see the twig-like junior collapse in a heap, so that he could take the credit for building her back up, for creating the perfect dancer. She never collapsed. Liz knew Lucy had hidden reserves that meant she gave a hundred per cent to each performance, whether the lead in *The Tin Soldier*, or an extra field mouse in a Beatrix Potter tribute.

But Liz had always felt protective of Lucy. She had quickly shifted her into the spare room of her Kilburn High Road flat, and soon discovered that Lucy's confidence and strength in her professional career did not transfer so well to her personal life. She seemed oblivious to the boys who brought her drinks at the bar, who hovered nearby, attempting to find the confidence to talk to her. It wasn't that she was too shy – rather she had settled for a man who Liz knew for a fact was never going to give her his all. But it didn't matter what Liz said; Lucy had been determined to make do with what she had.

Liz dug around in her bedside drawer for the half-packet of Minstrels she knew were there somewhere. *She always denied wanting more,* Liz thought, as she crunched the candy shell and sucked the chocolate inside. *She had every right to sleep with whoever she wanted, but she never did.* Liz had always thought it was a bad idea putting all your eggs in someone else's basket. But Lucy wasn't interested in anyone else. *She was always waiting.*

"And now, I feel like she's fallen into bed with the next available bloke," she tells her mum over the telephone. "She's on the rebound."

"Everyone's different, love – romance is complicated."

"It's just that she was going over there to get to know her dad, but all she'll say is her dad is away on business and that she's fine with that, even though I can tell she's not, and now she has this Ethan. She's been there a month and she hasn't seen a thing."

"Are you worried this Ethan bloke is bad for her?" Liz's mother asks.

"No, blast it. When she talks about him, she sounds happier than ever," Liz sighs. "I just don't want her to regret not taking this opportunity. I loved my year off. America was incredible. I saw so much and met so many people – I just don't want her to miss out. To settle for something before she's checked out the other options!"

"But she's not you, love, she's Lucy. You gave her a home and a friend when she was all alone. You taught her to cook – and remember when you both went away for the first time together to Ibiza? How you thought you'd meet James Blunt and you argued about who was going to marry him?"

Liz closes her eyes and she can feel the heat of the sun, the tight lines of elastic hugging her bikini to her skin as she stretched out on the beach. She can feel those sweaty, steamy nights under her skin, where dancing was loose, free-flowing motion, where they could let go of the structure, let themselves be washed away in the throbbing waves of people moving around them.

"Are you still there, love?" Liz opens her eyes and a muted Fry is laughing silently on the television screen.

"I'm still here," she sighs. "I guess it's just frustrating."

"I know you miss taking care of Lucy, but you've got to let her do her own thing, Liz. I know you don't want her getting hurt, but Lucy has to work this one out on her own. These decisions are hers to make, and a few stuff-ups aren't going to ruin her. She's a good girl."

"I just wish I could be there, you know – maybe I should go over for a few weeks."

"NO." Liz's mum says firmly. "Elizabeth, you've got *Cinderella*! And you're up for the lead in *Snow White*. And it's Dad's birthday next month. Plus, your Visa bill arrived this morning and I see you've been keeping Top Shop in business again."

"Mum, stop opening my mail!"

"Well change your address, then!"

"I did – it's the bloody bank!"

"Well that's not the point. The point is you have a mortgage and a job and you can't go off to the other side of the world on a whim. Lucy needs this time. You are a wonderful friend, but you are also a little bit bossy, I've no idea where you get that, probably your father's side. Lucy has to live her own life, make her own decisions. Let her do it her own way."

Liz grumbles that her mother is right, but it doesn't make it any easier.

"She'll be fine. You'll be fine. Now go to sleep."

"Thanks, Mum."

"Any time. Pay your Visa bill. Good night."

Liz rolls her eyes and pokes her tongue out at Mr Fry. *I know she'll be fine. But I do miss her. I miss us.* Liz turns the television off

"Nighty-night Lucy-Lou," she says, with a quiet knock on the wall. She closes her eyes and pretends the empty room through the wall is as it was before, that a quiet knock is returned.

Nighty-night Lizzy.

Ethan drives them out past Eastbourne. As they zip along the road, tracing the edge of the seashore, Lucy tells Ethan about Liz. How on the first day of rehearsal, at nineteen years old, the director had looked Lucy up and down with such distaste that she had almost run crying from the studio and never returned. But Liz had taken charge, had shown her where to put her things, where the best coffee was served. She had introduced her to her fellow cast members, whispered little warnings in her ear about those whose egos or reputations preceded them.

Two weeks into rehearsals Liz had found out about the two-hour tube and train trek Lucy was doing daily to her mother's friend's house out in Epping.

"Zone bloody Six!" Lucy told Ethan. "So Liz insisted I move into her flat with her on Kilburn High Road. And that's where we've been ever since," Lucy says. "Well, until now."

Ethan keeps his eyes on the road, but pats her knee to show he is listening.

"You see, I've sort of grown up with Liz," Lucy explains. "Most of my late teens and twenties have been spent in the cosy single bedroom of her flat. Popping up to Tesco for our milk and biscuits. Heading to the Black Lion for a shandy in summer or a Baileys in winter." There is a thought forming somewhere in the back of Lucy's mind as she watches the yachts stretched across the harbour and thinks of her old life on the other side of the earth. *I've really been quite forward, quite daring. The Lucy from London is quite unrecognisable. I'm on the other side of the world, I've gone and found myself a good-looking bloke – who I'm totally sort of living with, having not made any real effort to find anywhere else. It's like a new me!*

But does Ethan know you, Lucy? All of you? Well it's only been a few weeks, we're sort of taking things slowly, Lucy justifies to herself as Ethan slows and stops at a pedestrian crossing, letting a little girl with a giant ice cream walk carefully across the road in front of him.

There maybe a few things we haven't talked about yet, but really they are things from the past, and right now they just don't seem important. I'm just enjoying the here and now. The new Lucy.

But what is the little prickle of fear that sneaks along her back? She shivers involuntarily.

"Too cold?" Ethan asks, fiddling with the air conditioning.

"No it's fine, it's good," Lucy says. She shakes it off.

Look how the sun is making the water twinkle. Sad stories and complicated situations are not for today. I want to enjoy being with Ethan. The other stuff will still be there later.

They park and walk. Seven kilometres of chatter and natter about everything and nothing. Cricket scores and fish and chip orders. Lucy likes a hot dog with her chips, and gives Ethan a shove when he lifts his eyebrows suggestively. She has tried a deep-fried Mars bar and wouldn't recommend it. Ethan likes his fish battered, not crumbed. He has seen that Nigella woman on the telly do a deep fried Bounty bar and wonders if he should buy a deep fryer.

They swap beach sand for stony track, and Ethan tells Lucy a long, detailed story about the time he tried to dye his hair blonde at home when he was fifteen.

"My mate's sister had written down instructions on how to mix the bleach." Ethan shakes his head at the memory. "I went to the local swimming pool the next day with my mates and by teatime it was green! Dad got the clippers out and shaved the whole lot off."

Lucy tells Ethan about Hannah Stevens, who lived on a farm and came to school in a dirty Land Rover every day with a large Irish Wolfhound called Tim, who took up the whole back seat. Lucy tells the story of how Hannah had insisted Lucy was to ask Santa for a pony for Christmas.

"I went to bed quite terrified," Lucy laughs. "Horses have always scared me a wee bit. So I prayed to God to tell Santa I didn't actually want a pony, that he could give one to Hannah Stevens, and then when I woke up on Christmas morning I was completely sure both God and Santa were real, because I got the KerPlunk game I had actually wanted all along, and there wasn't a pony in sight!"

The rim of Ethan's cap is damp from sweat when they reach the base.

"Pencarrow Lighthouse. We made it!" Lucy puffs, exhausted from both walking and talking. The lighthouse rises above the rocks, and a welcome sea breeze blows gently around them. Lucy follows Ethan to the imposing structure and stretches her arms around the old whitewashed wall, its surface cool on her cheek.

Lucy and Ethan find a comfortable spot in the long grass and sit side by side, legs touching. They share a lunchbox, stuffing French bread with shavings of ham and wedges of brie that they pull apart with their hands, neither having thought to pack any cutlery. There are strawberries and blueberries that are only a little squashy, as well as a little bag of chocolate chip biscuits.

When their appetites are sated, they explore their surroundings, this way and that, looking up until their necks hurt and out across the harbour as far as their eyes can see.

"Actually," Ethan says, pinching Lucy's bum and kissing her softly on the neck. "I think I might quite like to live in a lighthouse. It's not just the design and the effort and the, well... the science, that goes into these things – it's their history. They have strong bones, you know?" And Lucy nods.

"Let's live in a lighthouse then, and when I'm old and rickety, we can have a stair-lift put in." Ethan screws up his nose in thought.

"Hmmm," Ethan muses, "I'm not sure I'll be wanting you when you're rickety." He accepts a pinch and a punch, then pulls her in for a long and forceful kiss.

They wander off again. There is a small grave surrounded by a white fence and Lucy listens, her eyes blurred behind a sea of tears as Ethan explains that, in the early days, lighthouse keepers and their families were forced to live in conditions that were truly awful. The houses were very basic – neither rain nor waterproof. Help for a sick child was hours away, on horseback or by boat.

"Her poor mum," Lucy whispers, her hand rubbing gently over the wooden railing. Together they find some hardy flowers – a few daisies and something pink. She takes the twist-tie from the bag with the biscuits and binds the flowers together in a little posy, twisting them onto the wire fence. Lucy says a Hail Mary, as her gran had taught her years before, pleased to have remembered the words. She watches the flowers dance in the breeze.

Their walk back is less strenuous. Ethan skims stones, while Lucy collects pieces of grey and green sea-glass. They walk a beaten path and talk about work. Lucy tells Ethan about a troublesome parent who is determined to produce a ballet starlet.

"The issue being that the little angel would rather be anywhere else," Lucy explains, "to the point of removing her pink leotard, telling me 'pink sucks', then running round in her underpants in the middle of the lesson!"

Ethan tells her about the house he's working on: how much he has enjoyed the personal nature of the project, the creative brief. The owners, who are open to new ideas and green technologies.

"I always thought skyscrapers were my thing," he muses.

"Sounds like you've found a new thing," Lucy says.

Ethan thinks it is probably the right time to mention Dubai; it's on the tip of his tongue. *But it's not confirmed yet,* he tells himself. He doesn't want to think about the dotted line on which he'll be asked to sign in the coming weeks. It would ruin what has been a perfect day.

"What about Georgie and Chris, eh?" Ethan enquires instead, taking Lucy's hand and swinging it happily in his own.

"Do you think they'll ever figure it out?" Lucy asks.

Chapter Thirteen

Lucy and Ethan fall into a gentle routine as March moves into April and April eases into autumnal May. The days grow shorter, the temperatures lower, and though the daylight hours shorten, Lucy and Ethan begin to venture out from their double bubble. Though they are still wrapped up in each other, Ethan's friends – who are now Lucy's friends – are an integral part of their winter routines.

Lucy shares the cooking with Georgie and Ethan and has set up an automatic payment for her rent each fortnight. Every Tuesday night, the three flatmates tumble down the steps, usually running late, and meet Jamie and Fran at One Red Dog.

"The old one on Blair Street," Lucy explains to Liz, though she has never actually been to the new one on the waterfront. But she knows it wouldn't be as good.

"Jamie and Fran are simply lovely," she tells Liz. "Jamie doesn't have much of a filter, though, so the things that come out of his mouth!" Liz pretends to be mortified but it's clear she loves him madly.

Georgie, who Lucy already thinks of as more than a flatmate, is a classic extrovert.

"You and her would get on like a house on fire," Lucy tells Liz.

Where Lucy tiptoes, Georgie stomps about. Where Lucy will

potter and hum while she empties the dishwasher and folds the washing, Georgie clatters and clangs and sings loudly. Lucy, who is used to the structure and timing of her dancing, thinks it quite mad to find Georgie up at three in the morning working on a jigsaw puzzle or fast asleep in her dark room at two o'clock on a sunny afternoon. But these differences have not prevented a firm friendship establishing. In fact, Georgie gives Lucy a confidence she sometimes struggles to find on her own.

On chilly afternoons, Georgie will bring hot chocolate and marshmallows from the local café to the draughty hall where Lucy corrals and coaxes little pixies and fairies into ballet first and second positions and pas de bourées, while their proud mothers watch on. And it's Georgie who will shush the chatty parents and tell them to pipe down, and encourages Lucy to do the same.

"Don't be afraid of them," Georgie prompts. "Tell them that if they want to jibber-jabber, they can do it at the café next door!" So Lucy does, and is surprised when they do as they are told.

Sometimes Lucy will climb out of Ethan's bed when she hears the creak of the front door opening in the middle of the night. She will slide into Georgie's bed with tea and Tim Tams, or Milo and Mint Slices, and she listens to Georgie lament the lack of decent men in the world.

"What about that Chris?" Lucy says one night, licking chocolate from her fingers. "He's a bit of a looker."

"We're BFFs," Georgie dismisses, "I mean he's, you know,

all right looking I guess." The colour rises a little in her cheeks. "But we're mates – it would be a bit weird, you know? I doubt he's even thought about it."

But Lucy is quite sure Chris has thought about it. He spends far too much time picking Georgie up and dropping her off places, and buying her fish and chips and lattes, to *not* have thought about it. She says as much to Ethan while they're supermarket shopping the next day.

"**B**anana's up, you think?" he grins, putting their own bunch facing down.

"What's it got to do with bananas?" she asks him.

"Ah, well. This supermarket we're in, it has special powers."

Lucy rolls her eyes as she tries to find a packet of strawberries that doesn't look pitiful. She's buying out of season, but she wants to make the strawberry shortcakes she found in a magazine a ballet mum had left in the hall.

"Go on then, tell me what these powers are."

"If you believe in such things, it is a long-held belief that if you come and do your shopping here at this supermarket on a Tuesday night, and you choose a bunch of bananas, and you place them curving upwards, then you are available and looking for lurve." He pauses to kiss her passionately beside the broccoli, making a couple of young girls cringe, and one of them suggests they 'get a room', as she elbows her way in to grab a bunch of broccolini.

"Now a couple of love birds like us," he says, pinching her bum less than discreetly, "we place our bananas curving down. Because we're already in love."

"We are, aren't we?" Lucy says.

"I'm inclined to think so," Ethan agrees.

"Love you," Ethan calls to Lucy, who has a head full of shampoo and a heart full of happiness.

"Love you, too," she calls back.

"I love you both," she hears Georgie call from the bedroom, "now shut the fuck up – I'm trying to sleep."

Lucy has boundless energy and a joy for life that she didn't know existed. Each morning she wakes up with Ethan's warm body beside her. And each morning they come together as the radio hosts laugh at each other's jokes or describe the day's weather, and she is lifted to a place so blissful that her cheeks glow and her eyes sparkle. She has even caught herself skipping on the way to work.

She has little time for texting, and only a vague interest in email. Communicating with the outside world is somewhat tiresome. Lucy sends one email to her father in Shanghai, telling him about her lovely Kiwi lad called Ethan. She provides weekly(ish) updates for her mother, in which she usually starts her sentences with "Ethan and I," or even worse, "Me and Ethan."

"You're nauseating," Liz sighs during one of their far too infrequent Skype calls. She can see the rosy glow in Lucy's cheeks, even with the poor quality of the camera on her phone. "You and your piles of sex with your Johnny Castle, your Mr Darcy, your Rupert Campbell Black."

"Rupert who?" Lucy asks.

"You've never read Jilly Cooper? Get thee to a library!"

But Lucy doesn't know where the library is, and she doesn't really care, for, right now, she feels her life has everything it needs.

Chapter Fourteen

Ethan is distracted. He turns his chair and sits with his back to his desk, staring out at the dreary grey sky hanging over the harbour. He thinks this morning's meeting went well. The Dubai people seemed impressed. There will be a Skype meeting with one other bigwig later next week. One last hurdle to jump. Ethan turns a pen slowly between his fingers.

What about Lucy? That was his immediate thought when he got back to his office, to the safe, soft cushion of his black leather swivel chair. Ethan has always been a sensible thinker. So he roots about in his bottom drawer and finds a chocolate nut bar. He returns to the misty morning view, unwraps his snack and crunches into the silence. Then he does what he is good at - he takes a step back from the situation and walks around it.

I have only known her for three months. But there's that overriding desire to be around her, and she is so much more than the fling things I've attempted before now. I say I love her and I'm surprised to find a new understanding of those words. Dubai has been around a lot longer than Lucy... but, there again, Ethan struggles to think of a woman who he's ever been so happy to have alongside him.

I really liked that Susan/Sally/Samantha girl. But then he really liked anyone in sixth form who'd let him feel her boobs.

I took that Belinda girl home for Easter a couple of years ago. But that was more because I felt sorry for her spending the weekend alone. And what a mistake! She spent the weekend complaining. The pigs were 'disgusting', the cell phone reception sucked, and she had no interest in either Monopoly by the fire, or fresh air and walking.

"Walking? Duh, this is my time off from the gym," Belinda had said, and gone back to her magazine and her black ('sigh') instant coffee. Ethan wasn't surprised that he'd not heard from her since he'd dropped her off outside her apartment and she'd told him he could have the chocolate Easter bunny his mother had bought specially for her.

"If I take it, I'll eat it," she'd said, to which Ethan had wanted to reply 'that's kind of the point'. But he'd instead said, "Right you are." She'd said, "I'll give you a call next week," and he'd said, "Yeah, sure."

He had then driven home to his house on the hill, where Georgie had stuffed her mouth full of the chocolate bunny and rolled around laughing as he relayed Belinda's refusal to join them outside by the bonfire in case her hair got smelly, and her attempts to work out why she couldn't find the E! Channel on the TV.

There was a time, in the first couple of weeks of living with Georgie, Ethan had considered making a move. Five years ago she'd replied to his flatmate wanted ad on Trade Me, and had been so forward about which room she wanted, what nights she would cook and how they'd share the chores because she wasn't going to be his damn housewife, that Ethan hadn't even thought to say no to her moving in.

They'd quickly settled into their home on the hill, and a friendship of shared rides to uni and work, and shopping at New World. Jamie had suggested if Ethan didn't make a move, he should set her free for others to try. Meaning himself. But Jamie had met Fran shortly after, and forgotten all about Ethan's bossy flatmate.

There had been one night of drunken fumbling at the bottom of the stairs, but by the time Ethan and Georgie had climbed the eighty-two steps they were both exhausted, and slightly more sober, and neither felt much like taking it any further.

Georgie had soon shacked up with a bouncer from the student bar, and Ethan had found he quite liked the freedom of not having a girlfriend. How odd it was for Ethan that he now found the idea of waking up alone in his bed a hazy memory. He swivels round to look out of his rain-splattered window.

There's only one question, really, Ethan decides, *and that's why haven't I told her about Dubai? That first night, when she was talking about Dubai, why didn't I say anything?*

He thinks maybe it's the same reason he hasn't mentioned it to Jamie and Fran, or even Georgie.

Because I don't want to worry them before I know for sure. They'd be anxious and they'd ask all kinds of questions. It's one thing to put on your best suit and tie and talk to a bunch of strangers in an interview about why you want to go to the other side of the world. You can talk of advances in career prospects and experiencing different working environments and cultures. It's easy to give the answer that, should you be so lucky as to be offered a position, then no, you would not be bringing a wife or children. That yes, you would be happy to work long hours and travel would be no problem – that you enjoy that side of the business. For, three months ago, when the questions were put to Ethan, they were all honest answers. But it's an entirely different prospect explaining to your closest friends that you are on the brink of accepting a job that will mean you won't see them for over a year, probably longer. *And it's even harder to find a way to approach that with Lucy.*

A small part of Ethan knows that once he tells people, then it's real. Once it's out there, there is no going back. He can't change his mind. *I'd look a right loser.*

"Fuck it," Ethan exclaims.

I've told Mum and Dad, he rationalises, *and the others, well, I really don't want to worry them all, not before I know for sure. It's not that I'm not being honest, I'm just holding back a little, so as not to cause a drama before it's necessary. Dubai,* Ethan justifies, *is in the hands of the men in the pinstriped suits with the Gucci sunglasses, the wide ties and the shiny shoes. I won't have the paperwork till later in the week, and there's no point getting people all worked up about it before then.*

Right now, it's business as usual for Ethan. *Live in the now. Who knows what will happen tomorrow anyway?*

But what about Lucy? The question nags at Ethan while he pretends to peruse a budget spreadsheet.

"Look," Ethan tells the numbers on the screen, "if I get offered the job, and if I can get a visa, then I might, maybe, be going to live on the other side of the world. And I'll cross that bridge when I come to it!"

He takes the lift down to the ground floor, and shivers in front of the caravan where a girl in a puffer jacket and scarf makes him a trim mochaccino.

"Who'd live in Wellington?" she laughs.

Chapter Fifteen

On the third day in June, they wake to a winter frost that has Lucy and Ethan humping and bumping against each other as much for warmth as for enjoyment.

"I should bloody well sort out the pill," Lucy groans as Ethan snakes a hand out and bangs about in the drawer that now stays well-stocked with condoms. Twelve packs, no less!

"You say that every bloody time," Ethan says, grabbing one buttock with his now freezing cold hand, making her shriek.

"Oh yeah, baby," he laughs, planting wet kisses all over her face until she throws herself under the blankets. "Yes, please!" Ethan says, smiling at the bobbing lump giggling under the blankets.

In the slightly sweaty afterglow, Lucy snuggles into Ethan and kisses gently along the length of his chin.

"It's all back to front," she complains, "this winter weather. I feel like I should be breaking out the Christmas decorations. I half expect Cliff Richard to be singing *Mistletoe and Wine* for me when I turn the radio on. But he's not." And though she is blissfully happy, she feels a wave of melancholy washing around her. She admits as much to Ethan, who wants to make her feel better, so kisses her for a very long time.

"Midwinter!" Ethan yells over the buzz of Lucy's hair dryer. He spits toothpaste in the sink and continues scrubbing thoughtfully. "Midwinter Christmas dinner," he yells again, returning his toothbrush to its holder beside Lucy's. "We can invite everyone. What do you think?"

Georgie is eating Weetbix and hot milk, shaking on extra spoonfuls of sugar with each mouthful. "No bloody bread left," she mumbles, taking a large gulp from her coffee. She nods along with Ethan and Lucy as they explain their plan to bring Christmas in the middle of the year to their little house on the hill.

"There's one of those plastic trees in the cupboard at work, I'll bring it home, shall I?" Georgie suggests.

"We can make decorations and paper chains," Lucy says, warming her hands on the teapot Ethan has placed in front of her.

"Paper chains?" Georgie asks, then quickly adds, "don't worry, don't care – so late."

"I'll catch a lift," Ethan says, grabbing his jacket and squashing a beanie down over his ears.

"We'll sort a menu tonight," Lucy calls out as they clatter and bang their way out through the front door, Ethan returning for his lunchbox and Georgie a moment after that for her car keys.

"It'll be perfect," Lucy smiles, sipping her tea and letting her feet dance ballet steps under the table.

Ethan arrives at work with pink cheeks, a large takeaway mochaccino – the cup stuffed with marshmallows – and a bacon butty.

"Breakfast of champions!" he tells the girl on reception,

who looks down at her slimmer's breakfast bar and feels quite miserable.

His good mood is momentarily frozen with the single click of the space bar on his keyboard. The bold black font announces a new email from the Aquiro Group in Dubai. His stomach takes a dive; he dithers for a moment, but moves his hand to the mouse and swallows hard as he clicks it.

When he opens the email, his smile quickly returns.

Delayed for three months. Will this be a problem for you?

And could you please read over the accompanying contract and sign if you are happy.

Absolutely no problem, he fires back. He prints off the email, collects the papers from the printer and staples them together with a loud clickety-clack.

A reprieve. Three months is a long time. Time with Lucy.

I can sign, and then I'll find the right time.

He works hard through morning tea, making sure he's prepared for the noon meeting with his clients on site at what will soon be their new home, and leaves the office with plenty of time to get there first so he can have a word with the builder.

By three in the afternoon, he is strolling back to the office. The clients were very pleased, as he knew they would be. Though it's a grey old day, Ethan is ensconced in midwinter Christmas dinner ideas. He'd quite like lamb, though it is expensive, and he's wondering if he should call his mum and see if she's got any Christmas crackers stuffed in the cupboard from last year. He doubts there'd be any in the shops.

What he is not expecting to find – after the lift pings open, and after he's stopped at the cooler for a drink of water, then meandered through the maze of desks and cubicles, through his office door – is Sharon, sitting at his desk.

Her hair is different: still perfectly straight, but it's shorter.

"Hello, sexy, shall we shag now or shall we shag later?" Her laughter replaces the sound of blood rushing through his ears.

Ethan realises he hasn't said anything and the seconds are ticking by, but he is trying to play catch-up. She stands, and he steps forward and kisses her lightly on the cheek, then steps back, giving himself some space.

"Welcome home, Shaz," he says at last, taking a seat on the opposite side of his desk, since she's sat back down in his swivel chair.

"Thanks, E," she smiles, running perfectly manicured fingernails over the width of his desk. Shazza's leather jacket is tight, and her boobs look like they're ready to bust out of their confinement in a tight pink lycra top. Ethan tries not to look flustered.

"Holiday?" he asks.

"Between jobs, actually. I've packed it in with Melbourne, done with serving cattle class. I got a place with a private airline in Dubai. Business jets, silver service, the rich and famous."

"Congratulations," Ethan says.

"Good timing, it seems." Sharon's eyebrows lift as she taps a silver polished nail on top of the papers he has stupidly left on his desk.

Upside down, Ethan reads the writing on the front page of the stapled document, and feels his stomach drop.

Aquiro Dubai Group
Contract
Private and Confidential.

Two things Shazza is not. Private or Confidential.

"Nothing's confirmed there," he rushes, "I'm not – it's not – for sure. It's not... public knowledge."

"Absolutely," Shazza winks. "Drinks tonight?" she asks. "The usual haunt?" She's collecting her bag and standing, smoothing non-existent wrinkles from her arse, which is squeezed into skin tight denim jeans.

"I, no, I... have plans." Ethan shakes his head to clear it. "I'm sort of... seeing someone now." He realises how lame it sounds. "Lucy, I'm seeing a girl – her name's Lucy."

"Serious?" Shazza asks, holding eye contact with Ethan, playing chicken. He looks away first.

"Yes, it is, sort of."

"Good for you," Sharon says, lightly kissing him on the cheek and pressing softly against him. "Still, we should catch up for a drink another night. I'm here for a week. Call me."

Ethan watches her leave. He sits for a long time, staring at his stapler.

Georgie has her back to Ethan, slicing courgettes into elongated ovals, ready to add to the stir fry. She stops every few moments to stir the sizzling chicken. He's been hovering back there for a couple of minutes now, and it's getting annoying.

"Spit it out, Ethan, or you'll get a slap with this here spatula." She holds it up in warning.

"Shazza's back. She came to see me at work, wanted to – you know, go for a drink."

Georgie paused for a moment, considering her options. Ethan is well aware she barely tolerates Shazza, and even that much is only to protect her friendship with him. The day Shazza had boarded the plane to Australia, Georgie had almost turned up with a goodbye and fuck off sign. But Ethan had a soft spot for Shazza that Georgie couldn't explain. Other than that he was thinking with his penis, as every single bloke was entitled to. But Ethan is no longer single.

"She's fucking with you, Ethan. Shazza's looking for someone loaded. She wants a big fuck-off diamond and a Mercedes E-Class Coupe. Said so herself plenty of times. Anyway, you have Lucy. So I hope you told her to fuck off."

"Uh huh," Ethan says.

Georgie stops chopping and spins around to face him.

"Don't fuck this up, Ethan. Lucy loves you, you love her, and I love both of you, together." Georgie takes the yellow capsicum and starts hacking pieces off. "She makes you sing in the shower and fold washing without being asked. Shazza plays games, Ethan. You know this, so don't get sucked in.

She's a bitch."

"Who's a bitch?" Lucy asks. Ethan and Georgie turn towards the door way where Lucy stands, swinging a tub of ice cream in a plastic bag, her winter coat gaping open over her pink ballet tights and black wrap skirt. Her cheeks are flushed and she sweeps her curls back from her face. As usual, they pay no attention and bounce back as before. Georgie sees a vulnerable young girl, and grips the knife tighter. Ethan thinks she looks beautiful and lovable, and he doesn't want to think about Sharon anymore.

"Why are you both staring at me?" Lucy asks, "Do I have chocolate on my face? It was only one Santé bar – I promise I didn't ruin my dinner. I'm starving. And you're burning the chicken."

Georgie starts throwing the veggies into the pan and, after carefully ramming the ice cream into a small gap in the freezer, Lucy follows Ethan through to the bedroom, where he's lying on the bed in his underpants, staring at the ceiling.

"Go on, then," Lucy teases, climbing on top of him and running her fingers lightly over his chest. "Who's a bitch?"

Ethan sighs. "Sharon. A sort of, fling-type thing I *used to* see." He emphasises the *used to,* and Lucy smiles.

"She came by work today, looking for..."

"A fling-type thing?" Lucy finishes for him.

"I guess so," Ethan says, flipping her over, so she is pressed beneath him.

"I sent her packing," he says, gently pulling her leotard down over each shoulder.

"I should think so," Lucy states, her own fingers sliding gently under the waistband of his pants.

Georgie can hear their laughter from the kitchen.

"You've got five bloody minutes till tea's ready, and close the bloody door!" The hall door slams shut and both Ethan and Lucy giggle. Georgie stomps around a bit, banging plates down and clattering utensils into the sink. But she smiles as well. "Shazza can go sit on someone else's," she squeezes the garlic press with gusto, "and rotate!"

Plans are afoot. Georgie calls Chris, who comes straight from the gym, and eats half a packet of Chocolate Thins while he's waiting for his bowl of ice cream. Chris says he has wine connections, a stack of bottles in his spare room waiting to be drunk.

"Social club has a wine raffle and Chris won it two years running," Georgie explains.

"*And* I have a keen interest in reading wine blogs," Chris defends himself.

Lamb is vetoed, both for length of cooking time and the cost, and though Ethan pouts, he is placated with a million kisses from Lucy to make up for it. They settle on chicken, the Jamie Oliver recipe with the pounds of butter and all the herbs.

"Roast potatoes, carrots, kumara."

"Beetroot, red onions."

"Peas!"

The list slowly grows.

"We've got to have a pav for pudding," Georgie says firmly,

writing it in capitals on the list.

"I make a great pavlova," Chris says, "it's a Christmas tradition at my place."

"Yes, please!" Georgie writes Chris's name next to pavlova on the list. He squashes himself on to the couch beside her and ruffles her hair.

"A pav for my princess," he teases.

"And you're a right royal pain in the arse!" Georgie smiles sweetly back.

"You guys are like an old married couple," Ethan says, licking the last of the ice cream from his bowl.

"Whatever," Georgie says, and pokes her tongue out at Lucy when she catches her eye and smiles.

Their four bodies are stretched out in various states of sleepy midweek satisfaction, with midwinter Christmas dinner plans all sewn up for Saturday night, and *Top Gear* on the telly. No one expects the knock at the door, and no one is keen to answer it.

"Next door've probably forgotten their key again," Ethan grumbles, rolling himself off the couch, making everyone else complain as they have to move legs and bums so he can get past.

But it's not next door needing their spare key.

The chill night air blows through to the lounge, causing outrage.

"Close the fucking door."

"It's freezing!"

"Bloody hell, what's going on?"

Ethan is left with no option but to invite her in.

She's sparkly, Lucy thinks, taking in her skin-tight pants and large breasts. She seems to have been sprinkled with pixie dust that catches the light from the lamp and makes her skin shimmer. Her heeled boots are this season, and Lucy wonders how she made it up the steps, and, more importantly, how will she get back down? Her smile is beautiful, and only creases slightly when Georgie says,

"Hey Shazza, long time no see."

"Hi, I'm Sharon," Shazza says, instead of replying to Georgie. She directs her full attention to Lucy, who wiggles up from where she was squashed into the corner of the couch. Conscious of her stay-at-home track pants and the splodge of chocolate ice cream on the front of her cardi, Lucy reaches up and shakes Sharon's perfectly manicured hand. Lucy's own nails are short and cut to the quick. She doesn't want to scratch the children during their lessons. The marked difference between the two girls adds to the sinking feeling in the pit of Lucy's stomach, and leaves her feeling tiny. Sharon, on the other hand, looks remarkably confident.

"Oh, a midwinter Christmas dinner, how darling!" Sharon says, picking up the list from the coffee table, and reading through the menu. "Is anyone invited?" Her question hangs a moment in the room. Georgie's eyes are wide with horror, her fingers find Chris's and squeeze hard.

"Ah, well..."Chris says. Ethan looks back and forth between Lucy and Sharon. Like a goldfish, he seems capable of little more than breathing in and out. His brain won't engage, other than to repeat in his head, over and over, *bloody hell, bloody hell, bloody hell*.

"Of course, if you'd like to come you'd be more than welcome." It is Lucy. Anything to break the awkward silence. She wishes Ethan would come back and sit beside her, but he hasn't moved from his spot beside the telly.

"Lovely," Sharon smiles, "I actually just popped up to drop back a couple of travel books I borrowed last year," and she places them in the centre of the coffee table, then balances the Christmas list on top. "I'd forgotten what a hike it is to get up here!"

"I'd forgotten what a hike it is to get up here!"

"I'd forgotten what a hike it is to get up here!"

"I'd forgotten what a hike it is to get up here!"

Lucy lies in bed, replaying Shazza's words in her head. *She's been up here!* Lucy wants to shake Ethan awake, find out exactly how often and in what capacity she has been *up here*, but his relaxed, calm sleep, his head pushing gently against her shoulder, goes some way to soothing her sense of unease. ***I'm*** *up here now.*

"I'm *up here* now," she says out loud and feels reassured. *So Sharon's a babe, with model-like legs and better boobs than Barbie. But she is the past. And though it seems,* Lucy thinks, *that the past is intent on clashing ever so slightly with the present, it is only for one night. Once this weekend is over, Sharon will be gone.*

"I'm up here now," she says again, closing her eyes and reaching for Ethan's hand under the duvet.

What about your own past? The thought floats gently past as Lucy drifts off to sleep. *If Ethan's past has come calling, what if your own decides to do the same?*

I'm getting to it, Lucy thinks. *Now I know Ethan and I are more than, more of... something – something lovely, I will find the right time and I'll tell him.*

Anyway, Lucy reasons, *my past is on the other side of the world. I doubt it will come knocking on our front door.*

But I'll get to it, I will.

Chapter Sixteen

Saturday does not dawn bright but Lucy, Ethan and Georgie are up early. One large expanse of grey cloud hangs like a dilapidated Austrian blind across the horizon.

"Perfect Christmas weather!" Lucy says, crunching on her Cornflakes and rising and falling on the balls of her feet, her toes sweeping circles on the carpet. Georgie and Ethan both mumble about proper coffee.

It may only be half past eight in the morning, but the fruit and vegetable market is already filling up. People carry floppy cotton bags that will be filled with the promised health and goodness of a multitude of seasonal produce. While Ethan and Georgie line up at the coffee cart, Lucy buys broccoli and potatoes. Georgie finds a buff-looking bloke in nothing but a red singlet and black shorts, who is selling the most beautiful bunches of baby carrots. Ethan insists on buying Brussels sprouts, though the girls insist no one will eat them. Georgie and Lucy spend a long time deciding on the chocolate for the trifle. They settle for a sixty per cent cacao almond praline, while Ethan staves off hunger with a Weiner sausage smothered in tomato sauce and mustard.

They meet Chris at ten at the French café on the Old Hutt Road, for a croissant and pain au chocolat, not to mention the warmth and the aromas of hot coffee and freshly baked bread. They smile and natter away the week's stresses, thumbing through the weekend *Dom Post* with buttery fingers, arguing over the weekend quiz.

"It's a takahe, I'm telling you."

"Dame Catherine Tizard was the first woman Governor-General."

"I told you a second-hand book dealer was a bibliopole!"

"I thought you were taking the mickey!"

Once home, Chris pops the cork on the first bottle of bubbles, and Lucy jiggles her iPod into its stereo cradle, and presses play with a turn, a twist and a flourish. *Mistletoe and Wine* fills the small flat, as does the merriment of four friends. They jostle for bench space, chopping and stuffing and pealing, stopping only to fight over the scissors and staples, as paper chains are draped along walls and fairy lights are strung across the windows. The tree stands, slightly crooked, but beautifully adorned in a collection of Lucy and Georgie's jewellery, some tinfoil stars and a collection of long-forgotten drinks umbrellas, adding a tropical Hawaiian motif to its Christmas splendour.

Around three in the afternoon, Chris declares he is starving, and someone pops a bag of microwave popcorn. They fold out the camping table they've borrowed from Chris's dad, butting it up against the dining room table so one long length crosses from the open plan kitchen/dining into the lounge. Jamie and Fran arrive, taking over in the kitchen, putting the final layers of plums and chocolate on their magnificent trifle. They fill the room with their happy arguing about who was supposed to call the plumber and why the pink wall is not staying pink, and who it was who said they liked it in the first place.

Georgie, Chris, Ethan and Lucy, each take their three-minute turn in the shower, and by quarter to seven, as Georgie pulls the golden, buttery chook from the oven, they are almost mad with hunger.

"It's got to rest," she insists, standing guard with the carving knife. Ten minutes – go and pull another Christmas cracker!"

"Something smells nice." Sharon has let herself in. Possibly she knocked, but in the tussle over the chicken and the crackers, and with Michael Bublé wishing them a very merry Christmas this year, they hadn't heard.

"Come in!" Chris calls jovially, "pull up a glass." It doesn't seem possible, but Lucy thinks Sharon is even shinier than the previous Wednesday night. She is wearing a classic short black shift dress that hugs her slender figure all the way up to the sweetheart neckline, from which her ample bosom threatens to bounce right out. Lucy watches Fran stand on Jamie's foot and he closes his gaping mouth.

"Nice to see you again, big boy," Sharon smiles, wriggling into Jamie for a kiss and a cuddle.

"What brings you back to Welly?" Jamie asks, and Ethan's heart beats hard in his chest. He hasn't mentioned Dubai to Lucy yet; he hasn't found the right opportunity.

"Between jobs," Sharon says, "I've chucked in Melbourne

and I'm off to Dubai next week. Corporate flight attendant on a private business jet. Short trips around the Middle East, as well as the usual London, Paris, Morocco. Car and apartment included."

"Other side of the world, eh," Jamie says.

"Not far enough," Georgie murmurs as she transfers the chicken to the serving platter. Sharon looks directly at Ethan and smiles, "I won't be alone though, will I, Ethan?"

"Lovely dress, Shazza," Chris interrupts, placing a glass of sparkling wine in her hand. "Stunning, almost like it's spray-painted on."

"Grub's up," Georgie calls. "Hurry up and grab a seat. You snooze, you lose."

"You okay?" Lucy asks Ethan, taking her seat.

"Sure," Ethan nods, "let's carve this baby up!"

I'm talking to her tonight. I'll tell her about Dubai. Suddenly Ethan realises how silly he is being. They will work it out. Maybe she could visit Dubai, or they could manage long distance. It wouldn't be easy, but he watches as she dunks her roast potato in gravy and puts the whole thing in her mouth.

"Delicious!" she mumbles through a mouthful of food.

I love her. I really do love her. She can come with me. If she wants to.

"I love you," he whispers in her ear, kissing her gently on the neck.

"I love you, too," she smiles, "now eat your Brussels sprout."

Ethan is a little quieter than usual, and Lucy feels a little awkward in her new skinny jeans and the soft red velvet jacket that she had seen in the window of a small shop in Cuba Street and thought absolutely perfect – until the moment Shazza walked into the room. But, sitting beside Ethan, she feels happy, and the vibe in the little house on the hill is a good one. Settled into their plastic outdoor and canvas camping chairs, they pull crackers, don their red and green party hats and call out their jokes.

"What do angry mice send each other at Christmas? Cross mice cards!"

"What do you get when you cross a lion with a snowman? Frostbite!"

They are imbued with wine and sated with perfectly roasted chicken, dunking their crunchy roast potatoes in perfectly browned gravy and each attempting to outdo the next with ever more delighted and delicious noises of appreciation, as they each eat the one Brussels sprout Ethan insisted they have on their plates.

Ethan holds Lucy's hand under the table, and she leans happily into him, watching Georgie across the table, noting that Chris has his arm draped over her shoulder. Whether it is the wine or the song, or the fact that she is seated in a low pink canvas camping chair, two seats down, Lucy has almost forgotten Sharon is even there.

It doesn't bother her that when Fran brings out the triumphant trifle to joyful hoots and cheers, and Lucy offers Shazza a pudding bowl, she is politely declined.

"I don't do dessert, darling." Lucy accepts an extra-large spoonful of trifle and eats every last crumb.

They lie in various states of delightful fullness. Jamie has popped the button on his jeans and leans against the wall with Fran's sleepy head resting on a pillow in his lap. Georgie and Chris have turned their camping chairs to face each other, and loll happily with feet in each other's lap. Lucy has claimed her corner of the couch, and having tucked her feet under Ethan's thighs to warm them up, she is dozing happily in the glow of the twenty tea-light candles that Georgie insisted on lighting. They flicker from every bench and surface and fill the room with gentle light.

Sharon is the only one upright, browsing through the bookcase.

"You really do love buying travel books, E." Her laugh tinkles over the group, "Escape to Egypt, Meals in Morocco," She pulls the Dubai guide from the shelf and flicks through the pages. "Great that you'll actually get to use this one. Isn't it fabulous we'll be there at the same time? It's like fate or something! You can be my bodyguard at the gold souks," she laughs.

It takes Ethan less than half a moment to realise how crazy he was to think that she wouldn't say anything. That definitely isn't how Shazza plays.

"Oops," she says, her eyes sparkling, "I wasn't meant to say anything, was I? I've ruined the surprise!"

Ethan knows this makes it worse. Everyone is waiting for him to say something. Everyone is looking at him. Everyone except Lucy, whose eyes are cast down as she runs her thumb over the soft velvet of her jacket.

A placement, in Dubai.

Not for another three months.

Great opportunity.

But nothing in concrete.

Lucy hears snippets of his conversation, of the others saying, 'wow', and 'congrats, big guy', and 'totally deserved, what you've always wanted'. But she doesn't trust herself to join the conversation.

I didn't know it's what he's always wanted. Why hasn't he said something? Why would he not have told me? Questions roll round in her mind, but she doesn't want to ask them here, in front of everyone. She doesn't want to admit that behind their incredible togetherness, Ethan has been holding back something of such importance, something that could pull them apart.

Long distance never works, I read it in Cosmo. And he'll be there with her. With Shiny Shazza and her pert boobs and her fancy corporate travel job.

Ethan taps her on the leg, breaking her train of thought.

"Lucy?"

"Just popping to the loo," she smiles brightly.

Lucy washes her hands very carefully, pumping the honey and lavender soap from its container with exaggerated carefulness, then watching as the bubbles form on her hands. She breathes purposefully, so as not to cry. She does not understand.

Why would he tell her, and not me? Lucy dries each hand carefully on the fluffy white hand towel.

When she opens the door he is standing there, his face lined with worries she is not prepared to kiss away. She looks at his shoes. Green sneakers with white laces. Blue jeans with a black belt, a pale blue T-shirt with a checked grey and blue shirt open over top, rolled up at the sleeves.

"Will you look at me?" he asks. But she only makes it as far as his neck, before her eyes return to his shoes.

"Dubai. With Sharon," She says. *Why didn't you tell me?*

"Not *with* Sharon," he says, "I didn't even know she was going."

"Right." Lucy says. *So why didn't you tell me?*

"I'm sorry – I was going to tell you. I was trying to find the right opportunity. Sharon just couldn't help herself."

Helping herself to you, Lucy thinks.

"This isn't about Sharon – it's nothing to do with her. I don't have to go."

"Wanderlust," is all Lucy says.

Ethan is getting frustrated. She won't look at him.

"What are you talking about?" He wants to reach for her hand but she's got them firmly knotted together.

"A strong, impulsive desire to travel."

"But that's not it."

"It's okay." *It's not okay!*

"It's not okay."

"I'm supposed to be travelling anyway, seeing New Zealand."

Ethan folds his arms across his chest,

"Am I holding you back then?"

"Well, not exactly." Lucy does not know why she said it like that, when she should be saying *I want to see New Zealand with you, or I'd be happy not to see any of it, and just stay here, in this little flat on the hill, with you.*

But she is hurt, and she can hear Sharon chatting through the lounge door about night time safari rides and twenty-four carat gold. Lucy has been to Dubai once, for a ballet performance. She spent three days between the theatre and a hotel room on the thirty-second floor of a hotel with the world's biggest Christmas tree. The closest she got to precious metals were the gold plated pillars in the hotel foyer.

"How, exactly, then?" he asks.

"Maybe its fate, like Sharon said." Lucy shrugs. "You'll go to Dubai. I'll go to the South Island."

"Wanderlust." Ethan's voice drips with sarcasm.

You did this, Lucy thinks, *how dare you be angry at me, this was all your doing, you and your sexy Shazza and your little secrets.*

"Come on, you two, we're going to the pub down the road. Karaoke! Taxi in two minutes." Shazza stands in the door way expectantly.

"We'll give it a miss," Ethan states, but Lucy is not ready for whatever it is that's coming.

"Lovely!" she says, "I'll pop my lippy on. I'll meet you down the bottom of the steps," and she looks defiantly into Ethan's eyes. He glares back with an intensity that almost breaks her, but suddenly it is gone.

"Whatever," he sighs.

Lucy sits on the side of the bed, rolling her lipstick between her hands.

"Are you coming, babe?" It's Georgie, and Lucy longs to fall into her friend's arms, to have someone friendly and familiar and on her side. But she can see that Georgie's hand is in someone else's. Chris, just behind the door, is waiting patiently. And Lucy doesn't want to ruin things.

"I think I had one too many reds," she says instead, "I can feel a migraine coming on. Think I'll take some paracetamol and sit this one out."

"Are you okay?" Georgie's concern is etched on her face.

No, I'm a mess.

"I'm fine, really."

"Shall I send Ethan back up?" Georgie asks.

"No, no, let him have fun with his mates," Lucy says, "tell him I'll see him later."

Lucy watches from the window as the two taxis pull away from the curb. She waits for footsteps, for the door to creak open, for Ethan to appear in the door way. She imagines him saying,

"I'm sorry. We're better than this. Let's just sit down and work this out."

But the steps remain silent, the door does not creak open, and Lucy is all alone.

Chapter Seventeen

Jamie presses the button and the taxi window slides down.

"She's not coming," Georgie says, jiggling on the spot to keep warm, "headache – she says for us to go on, she doesn't want to ruin our fun." Georgie stares at Ethan intently, as does Fran, who is squished between him and her husband in the middle of the back seat.

"Cool," Shazza says from the front seat, "let's get going then – time is money!" The taxi driver laughs heartily, and Ethan fixes his gaze on the back of the seat in front of him.

"See you there!" Jamie tells Georgie.

I tried, Ethan reasons with himself, *but she wouldn't talk. She's acting like I've been shagging Shazza, like we have some secret plan, which isn't true. If she'd let me explain, but she wouldn't.* Sharon sings along to a song on the radio, her fingers click in time with the beat.

Shut up! Ethan wants to yell. *Be quiet. I can't think. Time. To cool off. That's all we need.* Ethan and Lucy have never had a fight before, not a proper one. They've only ever argued over the insignificant, like whether Jeremy Clarkson is a genius or a big old twit, or about whose turn it is to clean the bathroom. Or whether Ethan is right that apple crumble can pass for breakfast food (apples, oats, a sprinkle of sugar, of course it can!).

What am I doing here? Ethan rests his head on the seat in front. In the pit of his stomach he knows he is responsible. *I should have been honest from the start.* He knows it's his own fault, but still, he'd like to shake Shazza and her big fat mouth. *Fix it, fix it, how am I going to fix it?*

"It'll be okay," Fran whispers, patting him on the back. "She's mad at you, but she's also mad *for* you. You'll work it out." Ethan nods, and hopes she is right.

The karaoke bar is packed, with a hen's night in full swing.

"Drink?" Jamie yells over the less than dulcet tones of someone singing *Barbie Girl*.

"One." Ethan yells back. Dutch courage, he decides. Something to light a fire, and spur him on, back home to Lucy.

It wasn't exactly like Sharon had ever really liked Georgie – *too brash*, and Jamie and Fran – *just so suburban*. But she'd felt quite smug on the taxi ride to the pub. Had smiled coyly over her vodka and soda, fully expecting Ethan to return her lust-filled looks, that a few hours from now she'd be in her hotel room with Ethan shagging her senseless. But he'd stared at her for a while then looked away. *What was that?*

I don't feel guilty. Not my fault he was keeping secrets, she decides, pulling up her tights.

"Fuck, I've ripped 'em." Sharon's voice is loud when she's drunk. She can hear the girls outside laughing, but she doesn't care. In the face of Ethan's lack of interest, Sharon had hit the bar hard. Countless kamikaze shots she'd planned on sharing have been downed solo, in quick succession, and she stumbles as she tries to stab her hotel key card into the toilet door.

"Le'me out," she calls.

"Open the fucking door, you slapper," someone replies.

"It's nor worrrrking," she says.

"Shazza? Is that you?" Georgie and Fran stare at each other.

"You's gonna helps me right? My key won't wo*rrrr*k."

"Bloody hell, we've only been here half an hour," Fran sighs, "who's going over?"

In the end it was Georgie who managed to stand on the loo next door, and direct Shazza to turn the lock. A small curtsey to the cheering line of girls, then Georgie and Fran took an arm each and helped Sharon back to the bar.

"She's drunk," Georgie yells to Ethan, "and she's all yours!"

"Why is it my problem?" Ethan yells back.

"She's your buddy," Georgie throws back, sarcasm biting with her every word. "I'm sure you'll be very happy together." Georgie knows her loyalty should lie with Ethan, but she and Lucy have grown close these last few months, and she isn't at all impressed with Ethan's surprise travel announcement, or the fact he had left in the taxi without Lucy with hardly a backwards glance.

"You can think of it as practice for Dubai." She glares for a moment, turns on her heel, and leaves Ethan holding onto Sharon, who is barely standing, beside Fran, who is attempting to hide her amusement.

"Good luck!" Fran tells Ethan, "I'm off to find Jamie."

"I think I might be sick," Shazza slurs.

Ethan drags her towards the exit.

"Fucking great."

Chapter Eighteen

Lucy calls Liz. It is noon on a Saturday in London, and Liz is holed up with a pot of tea, a plate of Jaffa Cakes and a sea of newspapers.

"I don't know what to do," Lucy says for the millionth time. She has stacked the dishwasher, blown out the candles, packed up the camping chairs, folded down the table and the only thing stopping her from hoovering is that it is midnight and she doesn't want to wake the neighbours.

Liz can hear her friend's confusion. Lucy has twice run through the events of the night, and though Liz has not met Ethan, she feels that whoever this Shazza girl is, and however sparkly she might look, she sounds like a vindictive cow. She says as much to Lucy.

"Maybe I was wrong," Lucy sighs, "maybe this thing with Ethan was just a holiday fling, and I've read it all wrong."

"But he said he loved you, yes?"

"Yes."

"Do you want to give him to her? If it's just a holiday fling then really, your pride might be a bit dented, but no harm done? You could pack your rucksack up, shimmy on down to the bus depot and find yourself a new adventure."

Lucy is quiet.

"But if it's more than that, if you think Ethan is the one for you, and you dream of having cute little Ethan babies together, well I am a little perplexed at what you are doing talking to me, when you should be down at that pub, giving that Shazza tart a short sharp shift!"

"But she'll be in Dubai with him."

"But Dubai is in the distance, Lucy love – you sort out the here and now, and then you can work out the details of what happens later."

"I do love him, I do. I just don't know what to say, and she'll be there, and..."

"Listen here, cupcake. You get your little a*rrr*se," Liz says her 'r's like a pirate, which makes Lucy smile, "into a taxi, and you march on up there and you say, 'look here, I'm crazy madly in love with you and I was really pissed off at you but whatever it is that's going to happen, we'll work it out.' Then you kiss him."

"Then shag him senseless. Guys love that," a voice on Liz's end chimed in.

"Who said that?" Lucy asks.

"Evan. He stayed the night, but he's going home." Lucy's brain works quickly.

"Evan, trumpet player Evan? Fancy house and car, *has a wife* Evan?" Lucy is shocked.

"Yes, well, ex-wife," Liz says, "and as I said, he's going home."

"I'm not," Evan laughs in the background. "Why do you have a picture of Stephen Fry on the wall?"

"So what are you going to do?" Liz asks.

"I'm going to go. Now. I've put my lipstick on and I'm going to call a taxi."

"She's going!" Liz calls to Evan. "Text me," she instructs Lucy, "I'll be waiting by the phone."

Lucy runs over Liz's words in her head as the taxi indicates left to park and her stomach fills with butterflies.

"Sixteen dollars ninety," the taxi driver says, and Lucy hands him her credit card.

"Whatever happens, we'll work it out," Lucy repeats to herself.

"Wait, love, don't forget your card."

Lucy accepts it through the front passenger window, thanks the driver and takes a deep, calming breath. *Whatever happens, we'll work it out.*

But how will we work this out? For as Lucy turns, waiting for the traffic to clear so she can jaywalk across the road, a couple stumble from the front entrance of the pub, the neon sign above the door turning their faces pink, their arms wrapped around each other. They move, as if glued together, towards the taxi rank on the opposite side of the road. Lucy watches, her feet frozen to the curb, as the taxi that has just dropped her off makes an illegal U-turn and slides in beside the couple. The woman looks up at the guy and smiles sweetly. Then they kiss.

Lucy turns quickly, taking refuge in a convenience store selling bags of chips and cans of Coke and, as she fights back tears in the lolly aisle, she wishes with all her might that she was in the sweets aisle in Tesco and that somehow she could be transported back to London - where she could choose from Minstrels and Jelly Tots instead of Jaffas and Jelly Babies. She doesn't buy anything; she simply waits a while, then slides out into the night.

The taxi ride home is quick, and less than an hour after she left, she is back at the house on the hill, alone and cold. She makes a cup of tea that she doesn't drink. She sits on the couch until she hears a taxi pull up, then quickly moves into bed, pulling the duvet close around her, squeezing her eyes shut tight.

Ethan falls into bed, exhausted. He's half-carried Sharon back to her hotel room. She'd made it to the bathroom and vomited. She'd cried a bit and finally passed out. He'd moved the rubbish bin to her side, filled a glass of water for her, ignoring the small stack of condoms she'd obviously left out at the start of the evening, and got the hell out of there as fast as he could. Every second in that stuffy room he had cursed himself and his foolishness. Why hadn't he just told Lucy the truth? That he had agreed to Dubai, but that he wasn't sure it was what he wanted anymore.

He wants to wake her up, but she's bundled up, so snug beside him, and he is so tired, too tired to say everything he needs to, everything he wants to, to make it right. He needs to make things right. Instead he kisses the top of her head, and twirls a curl around his finger, letting it bounce off.

"I love you," he whispers, then closes his eyes and sleeps.

Chapter Nineteen

Lucy wakes early. The winter chill seeps through her bones as she quietly slides into her jeans, tucks her nighty in and slips her woollen jersey over her head.

Lucy places her key quietly on the kitchen bench. She turns away. The symbolism is too great, but the image of the abandoned key burns into her mind's eye and she blinks back tears and breathes in quick shallow movements as she sits on the front doorstep and ties the laces of her sneakers. She hefts her rucksack on her back.

I'm not running away, I'm making a lucky escape, she tells herself as she quietly moves down the stairs. At the bottom she is quite breathless, and steadies herself on a fence post.

"Bye-bye little house," she whispers, looking up to the still sleeping structure, blanketed in shade, its curtains drawn tightly behind its windows. She walks down the road to the bus stop.

Ethan sits on the couch holding the key. He barely looks up when Chris and Georgie stumble through the front door.

"Coffee," Georgie demands, "Chris only has that instant crap."

"I offered you a cappuccino," Chris says, elbowing her out of the way and pulling the milk from the fridge.

"Cappuccino my hairy arse," Georgie counters, "cappuccino

does not come in a sachet."

"Coffee snob," Chris declares, pulling her close, "and I am pleased to say your arse is far from hairy."

"Get off," Georgie squirms, cheeks flushed.

"Not till you kiss me."

"I don't do PDA."

Their banter floats somewhere in the periphery of Ethan's consciousness. They must have finally got it together, he realises. Lucy will be stoked.

"Fuck," he says, making a fist to cover the key in his hand. But when he unfurls his fingers it's still there.

"Lucy still sleeping?" Chris asks, clattering four coffee mugs on to the coffee table, then sauntering back to the kitchen. The jug whistles, as does Chris as he fills the coffee plunger with hot water, oblivious to Ethan and Georgie's stillness, their eyes locked on the key in Ethan's hand. Ethan can't speak, so just shakes his head a little.

"Coffee's up, get it while it's hot!" Chris says.

"Think I'll just nip to the loo," Georgie says, and disappears down the hall.

"I need a sugar hit," Chris asserts, his head disappearing behind the cupboard door. "Cameo Creams or, wow, you've got Jaffa Cakes, the right proper British ones. I assume we can thank Lucy for those. Which shall we partake of on this fine morning?"

"Either," Ethan says.

He watches Chris carry both packets and the plunger across from the kitchen to the lounge, then fill two mugs with warm thick black coffee. The fourth mug stares back at Ethan, cold and empty, and he can't think straight.

Where would she go? She doesn't know anyone. Why won't she answer her phone? What should I do?

Ethan's questions are answered sooner than he expected. Georgie stomps in, her eyes lock on Ethan's, and stay that way while she fills her mug with coffee and stuffs a Cameo Cream into her mouth, chewing quickly and swallowing hard.

"She saw you," she says, fighting not to reach over the table and punch him square on the nose.

"She saw me?" Ethan responds, "Saw me where?" Georgie sighs. She only talked to Lucy for a couple of minutes, and between sobs, she has managed to ascertain the most important details, most of which she now passes on.

"She got a taxi to the pub. To come find you. But when she got there you were leaving. Lips locked with Shazza, apparently.

"Fuck," Ethan says, putting his head in his hands.

"May as well have humped her in the street," Georgie adds. Lucy didn't actually say that, but Georgie wants to see him squirm.

"Aw mate, you didn't," Chris says, and Ethan lifts his head and glares hard. Chris is a good bloke, but he's about to come a cropper.

"No, Chris. I FUCKING DIDN'T."

"Don't yell at him," Georgie roars, "You've only got yourself to blame for this mess."

"Think I'll go for a bit of a walk," Chris says, "Sunday

papers, maybe a bit of bacon for a butty."

"It wasn't me," Ethan says, willing Georgie to believe him. He needs someone to know the truth, to understand.

"Are you saying Shazza was tickling someone else's tonsils? Someone who just happens to look like you?"

"No, I mean it was me, but it wasn't me *doing it*. She was pissed, you saw her – she couldn't stand up without me holding her up. Then just as we were getting in the taxi, I leaned forward to help her in and she just dived on me."

Georgie is quiet.

"I swear, Georgie, I wouldn't do that. I took her back to her hotel, I got her a rubbish bin to spew in and I left. End of."

Georgie sighs. He appears to be telling the truth. Ethan puts his head back in his hands.

"It's not me that needs convincing," Georgie says. "Why on earth did you keep all that Dubai stuff a secret? And then telling Shazza before you told Lucy. Talk about playing with fire." Georgie takes a Jaffa Cake and nibbles round the circle.

"Lucy is a thousand times better for you than Shazza, and a thousand times more in love with you."

"I know," Ethan says, "I don't know," he continues, his head still in his hands. "At the start it was all up in the air, nothing confirmed, and we'd just got together. Then suddenly I was committed, on both sides, and I was just waiting for the right time."

"And Shazza? How did she happen into this situation, aye?" Georgie dunks the middle part of the Jaffa Cake in her coffee and sucks.

"She helped herself to a memo on my desk."

"Bitch," Georgie says, "but it's still your own fault – you've really made a mess of this one."

They sit in silence for a while.

"Will she come back?" Ethan asks Georgie. *Of course she will,* Georgie answers in her head.

"I don't know," she tells Ethan, believing a bit of hard graft on his part is more than necessary.

"Do you know where she is?" Ethan asks.

"No," Georgie lies. "You'll have to call her."

"I did, she won't answer."

"Did you leave her a message?"

"No," Ethan admits, "I didn't know what to say."

"Well a message might be a start. Perhaps let her know that you didn't shag Shazza?"

"You're right." Ethan stands, he takes his cell phone from the kitchen counter and goes to his bedroom, closing the door behind him.

"Of course I'm right," Georgie says, retrieving the frying pan from the cupboard so it'll be hot for the bacon when Chris returns. "I always am."

Chapter Twenty

Lucy sits in the café on the fourth floor of Te Papa. The soft lighting and vast spaces of the museum are easy to get lost in. A pink and blue Britten motorcycle hovers overhead. She sips her tea and nibbles at a small pork pie. The clatter of cups and spoons, the comfortable padded seating, the free newspaper and the anonymity are all welcome distractions from the turbulence turning inside of Lucy. She sits a long time, filling her cup from the teapot twice more. She reads recipes in the Sunday magazine: spinach and goat's cheese frittatas and savoury pin-wheel scones. A man tells a funny story about his daughter's first day at school, and the weather for the week can be summed up in two words, *southerly* and *rain.*

When Lucy decides she has been sitting long enough, she finds herself pulled into Passports, a section of the museum she immediately feels an affinity with. She whiles away her time, diving into the lives of immigrants who sailed rough seas to give themselves, their children and their families a better life.

Gosh, they were so brave, Lucy thinks, *they left all they knew, and once they arrived they had to start from scratch, build something from nothing.*

Lucy wonders if she is not a little similar, without the harsh living conditions. She has left her life in London, seeking a new life in New Zealand. *But I haven't sought much – more just settled with someone I thought was... what exactly did I think he was? The one? The love of my life? The perfect man?*

"I just don't know anymore," Lucy tells Liz. She sits on her bed, back in the hostel where the man with the tuatara tattoo kindly refrained from commenting on her tear-stained face and gave her his best room, the one on the corner with the slight view of the harbour. But the view has gone unnoticed. Lucy's rucksack rests, unopened, on the floor by the door.

"I've listened to his message three times now, and Georgie texted to say that she believes him, that Shazza is a slapper-floozy who needs sorting out, and that she will do it for me, just say the word."

"I'll be in on that," Liz says. It is the middle of the night in London. The glow from the streetlights on Kilburn High Road are casting strange shadows across the wall of Liz's bedroom.

"I've texted her back to say thank you," Lucy says, "And thank *you*, as well, for offering."

There is a silence that Liz does not fill. She rummages in her drawer, pops a Minstrel in her mouth and sucks hard, giving Lucy a chance to organise her thoughts.

"I haven't called him – I think because, right now, I am lost for words. You see, Liz, I had built him up, my Ethan. In my mind he was someone who would never do something like this, who would never hurt me, who would protect me from the sleazy side of things, which I thought I'd had my fair share of. But suddenly I'm thrust into the climax of some B-rated romantic comedy, watching him kiss the pretty, sexy girl while I stand on the sidelines."

"I'm just disappointed, even though I know it's unfair. I know that every person is fallible, everyone makes mistakes, and I know I'm not exactly an open book, but I keep wondering, why didn't he tell me about Dubai? Why keep it a secret?"

Liz thinks these are good questions for Ethan, but she tries nonetheless to offer some answers.

"Maybe it was confidential? Maybe he was about to tell you and Shazza beat him to it? Maybe, dolly, it's like you say, he's just not perfect. And maybe you should have a wee wonder about why you haven't been completely honest, yourself?"

Lucy bristles.

"But my past is just that, long before - ancient history. It's not knocking on the door with a pair of fake boobs."

"I take your point," Liz says, "but if it's past tense, why are *you* so tense? Why haven't you gone back to your little house on the hill for a kiss and make up session? If it's ancient history, why have you never mentioned it? Maybe Ethan would understand much better how you feel, if he knew what had been before him?

Lucy hangs up with Liz and feels tired. She pulls the duvet over her legs and, though it is only three in the afternoon, she closes her eyes. Hot tears trickle for only a minute, then sleep takes over, and there is nothing. Nothing but a small girl under a duvet in a quiet empty room.

When Lucy's eyes flicker open, it is dark outside the

window, and for a moment she is disoriented. *Hostel,* she thinks, *Ethan.* The red light is flashing on her phone, and her heart aches with longing at the simple message.

I love you. Please come back.

I love you too, she types, and with only a slight hesitation, she hits send.
I want to go back. I want Ethan back.

Walking home from dairy, phone almost flat, will call you in five x

Lucy smiles at Ethan's reply. She goes to the loo and puts her shoes on, ready. She wants to go home. Home to Ethan.

She fidgets at seven minutes. Give him a chance to get up the steps. She checks her battery is charged after nine minutes. It's fully loaded. At eleven minutes she gives up waiting and calls his cell phone, but it goes to message. She stands at the window, watching the seconds creep by. At nineteen minutes her phone finally beeps.

Your husband phoned. Confirms he got the papers you sent.

Lucy swallows hard. She hits redial, but Ethan's phone goes straight to message again. The home phone only produces an engaged signal. *Georgie,* Lucy thinks, but Georgie also goes to message, and Lucy is suddenly all alone. All the friends she has made are linked to Ethan. Her father has sent her one short email, saying he won't be back for a few more weeks but if she needs anything, he can provide a Visa number.

She leaves her room at the hostel. Left leads to the bar where she met Ethan, so Lucy turns right, and eventually stumbles into a dimly lit pub with a bored-looking girl behind a small bar. *Nothing from the past*, Lucy thinks. Just the smell of sweaty men and a small flat-screen playing re-runs of The Bill.

"Dad's in charge of the box, sorry," the girl says, while pouring a large vodka and soda and sliding it across to Lucy. "He's a big fan of The Bill – I got him the box set for his birthday. Big mistake."

"I've never really watched it," Lucy says, taking a big mouthful. Sweet and dry, she swallows it down and takes another gulp.

"Ah, you're missing out," the girl winks. She slides over to serve an old man in brown corduroy pants and a tartan shirt.

Lucy picks a seat by the window and watches the cars roll past. She hasn't eaten since Te Papa, so she buys a packet of chips, which she doesn't call crisps, and a second vodka. Her lips are numb and her thoughts feel cushioned.

What right does he have? Him and his friend Shazza with her big boobs and her bigger mouth. Bloody hell, not husband, not even ex-husband, in the legal sense. It's all been annulled. And he's on the other side of the world, probably shagging his way through SW1!

"Same again, please!" Lucy calls out. *Ethan has it all. Good friends, family, a job in Dubai. What do I have? Just the same rucksack I packed when I left. Five months. I came here to find myself, to find my place. I should go do that. If Ethan doesn't want me, then I won't want him.*

"I don't need him," Lucy tells the girl behind the bar. She thinks she has had four drinks. Though it might be five. Everything feels and sounds like she is floating in a lovely soft bubble.

"Shall I call you a cab?" the girl asks.

"I'm just round the corner at the hostel," Lucy replies very slowly and carefully. She realises she is quite drunk, and doesn't want to alarm the girl. "I really don't need him. Men are like elephants. Lovely to look at, but who'd want to own one?" Lucy cries tears of laughter. She feels she has never been so funny. "I'm going to find myself," she says.

"Do you think you can find your way back to the hostel?" the girl looks doubtful. "We're about to close up."

"Sure, it's just a walk in the park," Lucy nods. For some inexplicable reason she then salutes the girl, and tips out on to the footpath.

Lucy is a little confused at the intersection. Had she crossed the road?

"This way," the girl from the bar says, jogging to catch up, and pointing down the road to where the hostel sign glows on the side of the building.

"Hey, it's you from the bar. Are you staying here too?" Lucy asks as they walk towards the hostel.

"No, just out for a Sunday stroll," she says, "come on,

sunshine, you'll be needing a big glass of water and a wee sleep."

"I don't have any friends here," Lucy explains, "not anymore. I had a boyfriend and a husband. *Ex-husband,* not a real one. I think I need to lie down."

Jamie sips his Diet Coke and watches as Ethan skulls his third malt whiskey, lining up the glasses in front of the four beer bottles he's already emptied.

"I'm sure there's a reasonable explanation," he tries, "I mean she's only twenty-something. Can't have been married that long."

"Pft," Ethan says. "I didn't do nothing, and she packed up and left. I didn't shag Shazza. I didn't."

"I know, mate," Jamie sighs, and discreetly texts Fran from under the bench they are propping up.

E in bad shape. Will get him home soon. Don't wait up xxx sowy

His wife's reply is simply a sad face, a succinct summing up of Ethan's situation.

"Married. With a husband. That's a pretty big secret." Ethan nods to Jamie who nods back.

"Ex-husband," Jamie says.

"Yes!" Ethan nods intently, "a secret husband. Who has a secret bloody husband? I mean, look at you and Fran. I bet you don't keep secrets from her."

"I paid full price for *Call of Duty – Black Ops 2* last year. I told her a bloke at work lent it to me." Jamie sighs, weighed down by the guilt.

"Now that's a secret worth having," Ethan slurs, clinking his glass against Jamie's.

"I can't believe she's married," Ethan says.

"*Was* married," Ethan reminds his friend. "Not anymore."

"I bet they consumed it."

"Err, consummated? The marriage?" Jamie asks.

"That's what I said."

"Right, well yes, I assume so."

"She'll probably go back to London, shack up with him and have lots of little *Bwitish* babies."

"And you'll be in Dubai?" Jamie asks, for his friend hasn't mentioned it, not since last night.

"Hell yeah. Why not, eh?" Ethan stops for a moment and looks deeply into Jamie's eyes. "Mate, I'm sowwy I never said anything – honestly mate, it wasn't a sure thing. They delayed it twice. Didn't want to get the hopes up."

"Your hopes up?" Jamie asks. "You didn't want to get your hopes up?"

"Well, yeah," Ethan says, resting his head in his hand for a moment. "I mean and yours and everyone's. I almost thought I might not go, you know. Lucy and stuff. The house I'm working on is fucking *bwilliant*." Ethan proceeded to fill the next fifteen minutes with a hard-to-understand, drunken barrage of window placements, roof heights and references to clean-*gween* technology. The planning he's done puts him right in the centre of the action and working with the clients and seeing their dreams become 'weality'.

"You've lost your 'r's, and you haven't talked like this since uni," Jamie comments, draining the last of his drink and, making eye contact with the barman, gestures to indicate it is time Ethan was cut off. The barman nods and places two large glasses of water in front of the lads, then returns to stacking the dishwasher.

"Are you sure about this Dubai thing?" Jamie asks. Ethan leans over the table, and Jamie can smell the liquor on his breath.

"It's Dubai, mate. Dubai. They've got like really fuck-off big stuff there. And camels."

"That's true," Jamie says.

"Juss me and a first-class ticket to Dubai." Ethan confirms.

"Let's get you home to Island Bay first, eh?" Jamie suggests, helping his friend off his chair and out to car.

Chapter Twenty-One

For a week after Lucy's disappearance, Ethan drinks. He gets up each morning and goes through the motions. Shower, shave and go to work. He does not miss appointments. He is calm and professional and throws himself into his project like a man possessed. He visits the work site daily, helping the labourers clear rubble and holding cables for the electrician. He claims to be seeing his project through in these, its last few weeks of development.

"Bloody project managers," the builders joke, "we do the hard stuff and they come in at the end for the glory." But Ethan brings them sausage rolls and pies, and each day he arrives he rolls up his sleeves and works as hard as anyone else.

Ethan is busy, and that's all he wants to be. He can't keep still in the office; his mind won't settle. He doesn't want to think about Lucy, about her husband, about what he and Lucy had together or if it was ever his. He is angry and hurt. But he held back truths as well, and when he looks at the situation from the outside, his reasonable side tells him he has no right to cast stones.

But there is no more Lucy, no more answers, and no way to reason away his feelings. So his feelings are put away, and as much as his days are filled with work, his nights are filled and fuelled with booze.

He goes to the pub on the waterfront. He bypasses beer and goes straight to the top shelf, straight to whisky, straight to drunk. Each nip that slips silently down is like a soft balm that soothes the edges of his rattled mind. The feelings that rattle his cage all day are cushioned in a cloud of scotch comfort, and eventually he is able to stumble into a taxi and climb the stairs to his bedroom, where he is able to sleep, not bothered by the empty space beside him.

"Hey there, stranger." Sharon pulls up a bar stool and asks for the cocktail menu. Ethan skulls his whisky and signals for another.

"No girlfriend tonight?" she asks. "Sex on the Beach, please, sir." She flashes a smile at the young barman, who fumbles about with her credit card. The red cranberry juice is the exact same colour as her lipstick, and as she slips the straw between her lips, Ethan knows exactly where this is heading.

Sharon does too. She was hoping for it last night, but by the time she arrived, he was stumbling to the taxi stand, too shagged to shag. She'd come earlier tonight.

"I never got a chance to say thank you for the other night. There's a lesson there somewhere, something along the lines of don't mix wine and vodka." Ethan shrugs away her apology.

"I thought you were shipping out this week?" he asks.

"Unscheduled maintenance on the aircraft. I've got an extra few days." Ethan shrugs, draining his glass again.

"I've got an excellent travel guide for Dubai." Sharon drains her own drink and stands. "It's in my room, if you want to come." She waits. Watches him stand.

"Why not?" Ethan says. *Why the fuck not.*

Just sex. Hard, fast and slippery, just how she likes it. She screams when she comes, grinding her hairless pussy hard against him.

"Fuck, you're good at that," she lies beside him, panting hard.

I have to go, Ethan thinks, his heart racing but not from carnal pursuits.

"I've an early start," he manages to say, willing his mind to focus as he sits on the side of the bed and puts each leg into his jeans, then zips himself up.

"No explanations necessary, sexy." Sharon runs a fingernail along his back. "You never disappoint." Ethan fights hard not to flinch at her touch.

"We're the same, you and me," Sharon sighs. "Fucking good friends." She lies back on the bed, her breasts buoyant, bouncing as she laughs. "Tomorrow's my last night. You've got my number if you want to wish me bon voyage."

"I've got a dinner thing," Ethan lies.

"No worries," Sharon sees him to the door, completely naked, kissing him lightly on each cheek. "I'll catch up with you in Dubai."

Ethan looks up at what was once a crumbling stone tower and feels a surge of pure happiness at what he has helped create. Tomorrow the owners will shift their belongings inside and make this house their own home. Now, though, for one last time, Ethan can stand in what will soon be a living room and marvel at how he, the owners, the architects and the builders have come together to revive what was once a decrepit, miserable pile of bricks and stones. With sensitivity and an understanding of the value in the old bones, they have turned this place into a warm and joyful hamlet. The green outer spaces beyond the reclaimed brick walls are as much a part of the private world they have created as the bespoke granite bench tops in the kitchen, the reclaimed timber book shelves in the library and the large curving staircase in the centre of the home. This community of rooms at times verges on indulgent, with the crystal chandelier in the bathroom and the heated lap pool, with its glass wall and timber finish. The full home heating control system, top of the line Italian espresso maker and ice cream freezer were installed entirely at the owner's direction. The warmth of the recycled brick and stone walls, the soft curving lines he has used his bare hands to help create, add softness to the opulence. *I did that,* Ethan thinks, feeling more than chuffed with his creation.

Ethan feels connected to this project, this space, in a way he never has before. It has been a year of hard graft, moving walls from inside the architect's head onto paper – and finally into the structure before him.

He stands on the deck, the midday sun shining above. The stillness of a warm winter's day envelops him, and he's tempted to remove his jacket. But it feels good to be so warm.

Days like this in Wellington are few and far between, so he keeps his jacket on, and perches on the corner of a stone wall. He stares out across the valley below. He closes his eyes, letting the sun work under his skin, and when he opens them again they are wet.

Ethan sits in the still silence, the only noise coming from his own ragged sobs. From the outside, everything looks so right. The architect has been nominated for an award, the clients are overjoyed, and tomorrow he will board a plane to Dubai, where his dream job awaits.

But what if the dream has altered, Ethan thinks, *what if my heart is not set on what was once the sole indicator of success? What if making it big is no longer the driving force. And if it's not - then what is?*

I don't know.

"I don't fucking know." Ethan wipes his tears away on his jacket sleeve and sniffs. He fills his lungs with air and stands, stretching his back.

"Steady on, now," he tells himself. *What else are you going to do? Dubai is just what you need. Fresh faces, fresh ideas, a fresh start. Warm weather, a lot of money and opportunities to travel.* He sounds like a travel brochure but he is striding now. Back through the gardens, closing the front gates so they clang loudly. *It'll be fine,* he decides, *just new job jitters. Everyone gets them.* "I'll be fine."

He straddles his scooter, and with one last look over his shoulder, he bids farewell to the old and ushers in the new.

Chapter Twenty-Two

Lucy hadn't thought to plan her escape, but when the opportunity is placed in her lap, she grasps it with both hands.

It was the day after she'd read Ethan's text. *Could it really only have been one day?* To Lucy, with nowhere to go and nowhere to be, it feels more like a week. Wrapped in her warmest clothes, she braves the elements and strays through the streets of Wellington, hoping the brisk wind will blow away at least a tiny bit of the emotional fug that engulfs her. That didn't happen, but her hangover eased.

It is bitterly cold. Lucy sips from a bottle of Diet Coke and walks over a wooden bridge, its odd angles and quirky cubbyholes going unnoticed. Civic Square is empty, save a few hardy pigeons that coo quietly when she throws her half-empty plastic Coke bottle in the rubbish bin. Their grey feathers are a reflection of the damp winter sky and Lucy's mood. Both the pigeons and Lucy twitch distractedly, until the chill of standing still becomes too much and Lucy has to move on.

She finds her way into the city library, where the smell of coffee and warm sausage rolls from the adjoining café makes her stomach rumble. She finds a table in a corner, and she sits facing the wall, defrosting her fingers on the warm coffee cup, and rubbing her cheeks till the feeling returns. She nibbles at the edges of the sausage roll, tearing small pieces from the pastry and letting them melt on her tongue, before giving up and pushing the plate away.

The children's section of the library has giant red beanbags, so Lucy sits reading *Milly Molly Mandy* books for goodness knows how long. It fills her with longing for her mother, and she wants to go back. Back to her childhood bed with the Laura Ashley quilt. To be tucked up under her mother's arm, with a promise of homemade bread and jam to send her off to sleep.

She returns the books to their shelf and runs her fingers back and forth along their plastic coated spines.

I should go home, she thinks, *back to England. It's the best thing to do. My father is here, but he's not really, and my great expectations with Ethan are gone, and I'm tired. I don't want to have to think anymore. So I'll go home.* Lucy shrugs back into her jacket and winds her scarf tightly around her neck.

But her departure is stalled at the library exit. An exodus of smiling young people disembarks from a large orange bus and attempts to enter the library, through the same automatic doors Lucy is trying to use to leave. A posse of people in puffer jackets fills the small foyer with different languages and laughter.

Lucy moves to the side of the foyer to wait while the group splits in two, some heading into the library to use the free WiFi, the others choosing coffee and cake over communication. She stands watching, admiring their backpacks hung with flags and badges and patches. They wear an array of T-shirts proclaiming themselves expert bungy jumpers, river rafters – even one that boldly asks, 'Who are you calling a sheep-shagger?'

When Lucy finally finds her feet, she stumbles out onto the footpath and stands in front of the bus, the word *Zest* in large white letters emblazoned on both the side of the orange bus and the front of the driver's orange T-shirt.

"You right, there?" he asks from behind dark sunglasses. "Can I help with anything?"

"I... I don't know," Lucy replies. "How do you, you know, get on the bus, so to speak?" He disappears inside the bus, then reappears a moment later with a pamphlet.

"Website is best," he explains. "They've got internet access back in the library – we do it all, really, from short trips to the whole shebang!" Lucy turns the glossy pamphlet over in her hand.

"Great, that's really great," she says.

"You're not from here," the driver declares. "I'm usually good with accents. It's UK-ish, isn't it?"

Lucy looked up and saw he's lifted his glasses onto the top of his head, revealing a pair of very kind brown eyes and incredibly bushy eyebrows.

"I was born here, raised in Scotland, lived in London, now I'm back in New Zealand for a bit."

"Seen much?" he asks, and Lucy shakes her head.

"Bout time you did then, eh?" he says. And Lucy says thank you, and that maybe he is right, 'eh'! She turns on her heels and marches back into the library.

Bring your zest for life

...for travel

...for adventure

we'll provide the rest!

It takes only minutes to book, pay with her Visa and confirm a seat on the Zesty Besty tour, the bus leaving Auckland two days later. Lucy googles cheap flights and in a matter of clicks, she is booked on the first flight from Wellington to Auckland the next morning, and her plan to return home is shelved.

She returns instead to her hostel, and spends the night folding and sorting clothes. She scavenges a box from reception, filling it with things she doesn't want to carry with her.

Lucy sits with her legs crossed, wedged between a pile of pants and a folded tower of t-shirts. She texts her father, a polite but brief request:

Call me please.

She holds her phone in her lap and waits.

"Hello, Lucy speaking."

"Yes, Lucy, I got your message."

"Hi. Dad. I'm going travelling. Around New Zealand."

"Good, yes, that's lovely," he says.

"I've got a box of things. Stuff I don't want to drag around. Can I leave them with you? At your place?"

"Of course. Sorry I've not been in touch. Are you going with the Ethan fellow?"

Lucy regrets the impulsiveness of the email sent weeks ago.

"No."

"Are you okay?" her father asks.

"Oh yes, I'm grand," Lucy bites. "I travelled half way around the world to get to know my father, and he buggered off to Tokyo."

"Shanghai."

Lucy does not respond. She lets the silence linger.

"I'm sorry, Lucy, I didn't realise…"

"No, I guess not," Lucy sighs.

"I do want to see you, Lucy, I've just been stuck in Shanghai sorting out this mess – it's taken so much longer than I previously envisaged…"

"Look, don't worry," Lucy rushes. Fresh tears make her voice shaky. "I'll be fine. I really didn't mean to be rude, I mean I've hardly had time to get to know you, but it's not your fault I've broken up with my boyfriend."

"I guess I'm not the easiest man to pin down," her father muses.

"No." Lucy stares at the pile of scarves she has yet to untangle. "You're kind of elusive," she whispers.

"Mmm," her father responds, "just used to being on my own, I guess."

"And now I'm on my own as well," Lucy sniffs, "so we've something in common."

"Mmm," her father replies again. "Where exactly are you?"

"At a hostel on Taranaki Street."

"You know the Museum Hotel?" he asks.

"Yes," Lucy nods at the three pairs of ballet slippers resting by her rucksack.

"Leave your box at reception there. I'm back in Wellington for three days next week – there's a conference at the hotel. I'll pick it up then. I'm booking you a room for the tonight. A bit of comfort before all that bungy jumping and sightseeing."

"It's okay, Dad," Lucy says, "I'm sorry I yelled."

"I want you to go to the hotel," her father says. "Let me do this for you."

Lucy hauls her heavy body out of the oversized oval bath, and slides into a fluffy white robe. Her box is safely stowed at reception. Her rucksack is packed and ready.

All that is left of Lucy's Wellington life is to call her boss. She feels a tad selfish as she explains that she won't be able to continue with her dance classes, effective immediately. She accepts the dressing down, apologising profusely for the short notice, and agrees she is very lucky the school holidays will give the dance school time to find a replacement. The children will miss her, she is told. Lucy hangs up the phone and crawls into the closest of the two beds, using the corner of the sheet to catch the waterfall of tears she can no longer hold back.

"I'll miss so much," she sobs into her pillow. "I'll miss it all so much."

The first three days on the Zest bus take Lucy up to the top of the North Island. Between boogie-boarding down sand dunes and digging holes to find thermal springs at Hot Water Beach, Lucy checks her phone constantly. She pretends she is checking that her father had retrieved her box from the hotel, and that her mother has a copy of her itinerary, but the squeeze in her chest and the empty hollow in her stomach are renewed each time she sees that she has not missed a call or a text from Ethan.

In Rotorua, Lucy phones her mother, full of bravado and excitement having braved the fastest luge track.

"Did you have a helmet?" her mother asks. "Did you take photos? Are the other people on the bus nice? Don't do drugs, even if someone offers them free. Especially if someone offers them free." Her mother seems genuinely happy that Lucy is having such a good time. Liz however, is harder to convince.

"Have you talked to him?" she asks. "Does he even know where you are?"

"He doesn't want to know. He knows my number and he hasn't called me. And anyway, this isn't about him. It's not about boyfriends, or ex-husbands, or absent fathers either. It's just about me, Liz. I'm doing what I came here to do – what you told me to do. I'm having an adventure, being brave, getting out there and living life."

"But are you okay?" Liz asks.

"Other than being more hungover more times than I've ever been in my life, I'm fine."

I'm fine, Lucy tells herself every morning as she brushes her teeth and stuffs her belongings back into her pack. But Liz's concern has upset Lucy. She doesn't want to consider her travels as anything more than putting herself first for once, as anything more than being a single independent woman taking control of her life. So Lucy turns her unease to anger.

I'm not a totally hopeless case, I've got this far in my life, haven't I? Am I not doing new things, having fun, putting myself out there? I'm sick of worrying about what everyone else is thinking, and I'm sick of being worried about.

Lucy defiantly turns her phone off and stuffs it down the bottom of her rucksack.

A girl named Fritzi asks Lucy to sit beside her on the bus from Rotorua to Taupo.

"I am from Germany and I loves all things of the Westlife," Fritzi shares. With only minimal knowledge of the boy band, Lucy decides it best to agree that *World of Our Own* is one of their best songs, and is rewarded with a copy of Westlife's book, *Our Story,* to read.

"It's very sad," Fritzi says. "They are to breaking up. They are still loving each other, but they are doing the other things like on the television and the radio." Lucy provides a listening ear, agreeing that Shane (whoever he is) will definitely have a wonderful solo career.

Lake Taupo grabs their attention, and they are distracted by their driver Ben offering options of nature hikes, fishing trips, and jet boat rides. When they hop off the bus, Fritzi hugs Lucy tight. "You are nice girl. You come get the drunkenness with us." So Lucy gets the drunkenness, and continues to get it most nights, and sometimes during the day. Fritzi has no problem 'making the friends', which she insists is the whole point of the tour, and Lucy soon finds that with a bit of liquor-induced confidence, she too is able to dance on tables and sing karaoke.

Days merge into nights, then into new days, as Lucy throws herself into every activity available. River rafting, guitars around campfires – even a horse trek in Taihape on a geriatric pony called Polly, who stops to sniff and chew on anything hanging at head height. She steers clear of the bigger horses, overwhelmed by their long legs and the over-confident way they toss their manes. But she is brave enough to give Polly a quarter apple from her hand and leaves the stable smiling from ear to ear.

When the bus rolls into Wellington, Lucy can't believe it. She is back in Ethan territory and has arrived unprepared.

"You visit with your friends?" Fritzi asks, as they check into their hostel beside the railway station. Lucy has given Fritzi the edited version of her time in Wellington, explaining that she'd spent a few months working, catching up with her dad. And yes, she had met some lovely people, and she totally agrees that Kiwis really are ever so friendly.

"Maybe on the way back," Lucy says, and chooses instead to tuck up for an early night.

The boat ride the next morning is rough. The Cook Strait pounds their ferry with waves that take them up into the sky then crunch them back down, shuddering the boat and rocking them from side to side. Lucy barely manages to hold onto her breakfast, and she has never been so happy to return to dry land. Fritzi is less lucky, stumbling off clutching her sick bag, and Lucy quickly finds her some ginger beer to settle her stomach before the bus ride to the West Coast.

Seal colonies, pancake rocks, quad bike riding, helicopter rides, standing on a giant glacier, the majestic Milford Sounds, bungy jumping. Lucy ticks off each activity in her guide book. "I'm doing it all, Fritz!" she tells her friend. She embraces feelings of satisfaction and achievement, awash with the cool air of Fox Glacier and, though her fingers and toes are cold, her cheeks are flushed pink and her smile is genuine.

"How could not someone feel very happy here?" Fritzi demands to know. "It is perfect." And Lucy readily agrees.

I really do feel fine. Lucy checks her reflection as she peers over the edge of the safety rail on a platform jutting out over Lake Matheson. She pokes for a moment at her emotions. *Am I getting over it, or am I just getting on with it?* she wonders. The mountains and their upside down reflection pull her eyes to the far edge of the lake. She stands motionless, breathing slowly, her every breath visible in the cool morning air.

"Lucy. LUCY!" Ben, the driver, is waving from the deck that juts out from the café. "Breakfast's up babe!"

They drive on to Queenstown, napping and chatting and singing. Their small motley crew of personalities have started melding into a cohesive unit. Ben guides and goads them through an endless array of new activities. Samuel from Israel tells the best jokes. Mark is the shyest, but his quiet encouragement is what got Lucy onto the pony in Taihape.

Anita and Elaine from Scandinavia are bookworms, dumping clothes from their packs in favour of historical narratives and stories of lives lived throughout the length of New Zealand. They also have a never-ending supply of plasters and paracetamol, of hair pins and packets of raisins and peanuts. Fritzi is loud and loveable, and Jane and Eamon have the most delightful Irish accents – Lucy loves to listen to the couple bickering,

"Sure, what could be wrong with another one? They're only wee," Jane will say to Eamon when he suggests the forty or so fridge magnets they've already purchased are getting quite heavy in his pack. And he'll tell her, "If they're just wee, you can carry them yourself, like." Then they'll tussle outside and Eamon won't let her carry a thing. *They remind me of Georgie and Chris,* Lucy thinks.

That night – as she accepts a dare set by her fellow bus mates and dances the dying swan in the garden bar of a pub in Queenstown, wearing a Two Dollar Shop tutu – Lucy feels better than fine. *I'm happy,* Lucy thinks to herself. *I'm living one day at a time. I'm leaving the past behind me and I'm really, truly, totally not at all bothered about the future.* She stumbles into her bunk bed in the wee hours of the morning and can't be bothered taking her jeans off, so she pulls the duvet up and lets her head fall onto the soft pillow. *I'm a new version Lucy, Lucy 2.0* she giggles to herself, *and what's more, I can prove that I've moved on!* she decides.

Tom is American. He is short and stocky, young and pretty.

"He is like the Kian from Westlife," Fritzi elbows Lucy, "and he's all hots for you." Lucy hasn't realised, but now she spends the bus journey to Dunedin making it her job to notice. Tom smiles in her direction a lot, and in the numerous photo opportunities that present themselves, it seems he often finds a way to be beside her. Sometimes his arm finds its way around her waist but, then again, so does Fritzi's.

"He's too young for me." Lucy and Fritzi have finished their tour of the Speight's Brewery and are making the most of the product with their fellow Zesty travellers.

"You are not the old hag," Fritzi replies.

"I'm thirty next year. He looks about nineteen," Lucy whispers.

"He is twenty-one," Fritzi corrects her, "and I hear he is very, how you say, hanging big." Lucy almost chokes on her beer.

"Fritzi, you can't say that. You say he's well-endowed."

"I'm not meaning his money. I'm meaning his penis."

"Oh god," Lucy tries to hide behind her pint glass as the people at the table beside theirs snicker over their glasses of ale.

"Whose penis are we talking about?" someone calls out.

"That would be mine." Tom appears with a beer in each hand.

"One for you," he smiles, placing a glass in front of Lucy. Fritzi immediately hops off her stool.

"I am needing the bathroom." Fritzi waggles her eyebrows in Lucy's direction, stopping briefly behind Tom's back to make humping motions. Tom thinks Lucy's cheeks are the colour of summer raspberries, and he tells her as much, which makes her blush even more.

"Now they're red like a baboon's butt!" he laughs, clinking his beer glass to her own.

Though Lucy knows very little about Tom, as they slow dance in a corner of an anonymous bar somewhere in the deep south of New Zealand, she decides that this is exactly what she needs. He tells her he was born in Texas, raised on a ranch, and he admits that he's a bit of an American cliché. He has sandy blonde hair and baby blue eyes and his voice is warm and smooth when he asks thoughtful questions about Lucy: where she grew up, what made her come back to New Zealand. He listens intently while she talks about seeing her dad for the first time in years, and about her ballet days.

"Never been to a *bell-lay*," he says, holding her close, "but I'll stick it on my bucket list."

"I'm eight years older than you," Lucy says as his hand slides down her back, resting purposefully on the right cheek of her bum. "When I was learning to drive a car, you were probably learning to ride a bike."

"I drove my daddy's car when I was eleven," Tom explains, rocking gently into her, in time with the music. "I'm a fast learner."

After that, they don't talk much. Lucy can't work out when the dancing moved to kissing, but his lips are warm and his arms are muscular and strong. She is losing all sense of time and place and cares not a jot. The walk back to the hostel is slow, as Tom takes every opportunity to press her up against walls in dark corners. His lips and fingers are enchanting and every time he takes them away she has to stop herself begging for their return.

In the bright light of the hostel foyer, Tom tells her to 'wait there', and she does as she's told.

He's not Ethan. Lucy immediately works to shut down the thought. *Shut up,* she tells herself, *this is what I need, someone warm and sexy who wants me. No complications, just good old-fashioned fondling. I'm fine. I'm totally fine.*

Tom returns and, taking her face gently in his hands, he kisses her. His tongue gently searches for her own, till there are no thoughts left to think.

"I got us our own room," he whispers. Lucy smiles and nods.

I'm so much better than fine.

The room is dark but neither of them move to turn the light on.

"You're beautiful," Tom says, undoing the button of her jeans. "I've been staring at you from the other side of the bus, barely able to contain myself. You're so sexy, you know – when you're reading, you stick your tongue out a little between your lips. So sexy. I can't wait to make you come."

Lucy stifles a giggle. She blushes furiously but he gently lifts her chin so that her eyes lock on his.

"You might not realise it, but you've been driving me wild."

Lucy hasn't realised; she has barely paid attention to Tom. She knows he has a guitar, but not whether he's particularly good at playing it. But his hands are warm and firm when they find their way inside her pink cotton knickers.

"Good morning, Lucy," Fritzi calls, from inside her sleeping bag in the bunk room they were supposed to share. "How are you?"

"Fine, I'm fine," Lucy mumbles, her eyes stuck to the black and white chequered floor. She fumbles with the zip on her pack and digs around inside for her toilet bag. Her teeth are furry and she's desperate to scrub them.

"You not come home last night," Fritzi grins at her, as she brushes her long straight blonde hair and twisting it up into a French roll.

Lucy misses breakfast, preferring a long hot shower. In the quiet room she empties out her rucksack and starts to repack her belongings. She holds her cell phone, staring for a moment at the blank screen. When she turns it on, it beeps almost instantly. A text from Georgie makes her smile. She would like to ring and say how fantastic she thinks it is that Georgie and Chris are now together. But she just isn't ready. Not yet. She turns the phone back off and puts it back in the bottom of her bag, where the real world can stay buried.

At some stage, Lucy will have to deal with her real life and the people in it. *But not right now. Not yet. For now, I choose to forego the past, in favour of future fun and...*

"Fuck me, he sounds like the dream." Fritzi is staring at the back of Tom's head, which floats above the headrest, three rows from the front of the bus on the right hand side. Lucy elbows her.

"Stop staring, and don't be so loud."

"Did he really say you look like bum of the baboon? And this makes you horny?"

"Shhh," Lucy says again, covering her face with her hands.

"How much?" Fritzi asks, and Lucy whispers how many times they did it, and how he was ready for another go at six in the morning. She feels a bit hot and bothered remembering how he'd sat her on top of him, rocking gently in...

"Lucy, you stop the dreaming, I ask you, does it be big?" Lucy isn't sure what Fritzi means.

"Oh!" she remembers their conversation the night before. She puts her hands back over her face and nods.

"You are what they say – lucky, lucky girl. You will have the wedding and make beautiful babies," she sighs.

"God, no," Lucy says, shaking her head firmly. "He's far too young for me, I'm exhausted." She closes her eyes, but opens them quickly as an image of herself in a white satin wedding dress, smiling up at Ethan, burns into her brain. The emotions that come attached to the image quickly travel through to the rest of her body and her breath quickens. She grips the arm of her seat. *What did I do? What have I done?*

"You feel not well?" Fritzi asks. "Have some water." Lucy sips from her water bottle and breathes slowly, calming herself down. *I'm fine, I'm really fine. He doesn't want me, I don't need him. I'm fine. The past.*

"I think I better have a snooze," Lucy says, closing her eyes again, this time letting darkness engulf her. *I'm fine,* she thinks again, feeling her body relax and sleep come calling. *Just a bit tired. Not enough sleep. But I'm doing great. Just fine.*

Chapter Twenty-Three

"Bloody Lucy and Ethan. They're both as bad as each other," Georgie complains, dunking toast soldiers into a perfectly boiled egg. "You're going to make me fat."

"I'll still shag you," Chris says, munching on his own piece of toast while scanning the news websites on his laptop. "It's not like we set a good example – look how long it took us to sort it out." Georgie replies with a sigh.

"We're different – we had to get over the whole awkward friends thing."

"If I'd known all it would take was a couple of bottles of leg opener," Chris jokes, ducking just in time to miss the crust of Georgie's toast sailing past his head.

"Okay, *three* bottles. And anyway, I bet Lucy will call you when she's ready. I'm late for the gym," he says, grabbing his jacket and blowing her a kiss.

"Know-it-all," Georgie yells out.

"I'm making enchiladas for tea," he calls from the front door.

"I won't eat them," Georgie calls back, "I'm having salad." But she's already dreaming of their cheesy deliciousness.

Georgie pulls Chris's laptop over to her side of the table and logs in to Facebook. She goes straight to Lucy's page, finding Liz on her list of friends. Georgie and Liz have never met, never spoken, only ever been spoken about, but Georgie feels she has no choice. She quickly sends Liz a private message.

Less than half an hour later her phone is ringing.

"Not ex-husband," Liz explains, "annulment. But it's a long story and if Lucy hasn't explained, I don't..."

"It's okay," Georgie says. "I'm not stalking her or anything – I don't want to stick you in the middle. I just want to know she's not fallen under a bus and isn't lying in a coma in Wellington Hospital."

"She's fine," Liz says, tucking the phone into the crook of her neck and pulling her jacket more tightly round her middle. She's in dress rehearsals for Sleeping Beauty and if she gets caught in costume outside she'll get her arse kicked all the way to Cornwall. But she knows Georgie is worried, because she is worried too. "I mean, she's not *fine*, but she's determined to deal with this alone. She's on a bus somewhere in your godforsaken country, trying to be some kind of a swashbuckling girl about town, independent of spirit and of mind."

"That doesn't sound very Lucy," Georgie says.

"It's not at all very Lucy. But I've been told to mind my own beeswax, and from what I can tell she is in no danger, at least not physically. Emotionally, I'm not really sure what's going on. Shite - I have to get back inside, but let's talk again, call me if you hear from her and I'll do the same."

Georgie is pleased she's spoken to Liz. She calls Lucy's cell phone and leaves a message,

"Your friend Liz tells me you're on a bus somewhere in the wop wops, chasing wot wots, and that you haven't been run over by a tractor or struck by lightning and you're not lying in a coma being fed through a tube. These are all thoughts that have run through my mind. I hope you feel suitably guilty. Now I'm going to bugger off and leave you alone. I'm far too busy to be chasing around after you when I can be here at Chris's house shagging him senseless. See what you're missing? Now call or text or email or send me a fucking postcard. If you want to. I'm not that bothered."

"Do you think you should say something to him?" Fran asks. Her knees are aching but she's determined to make it right round the skirting board before she stops for a Kit Kat. *Think of the Kit Kat,* she tells herself as she dips her paintbrush into the bucket of eggshell coloured paint and shuffles a little further along the hard laundry floor.

"Like what?" Jamie asks from the ladder, where he's cutting in corners on the feature wall with the sage green paint that will go perfectly with Fran's *'they're not white, they're eggshell',* cane baskets.

"Well, what's he said? Does he miss her?"

"I'm going to hazard a guess, from the amount of liquor he's imbibing each night, that yes, he misses her. But I will also guess from the look of thunder that crosses his face, should her name come up in conversation, that he's not quite ready to get over the fact that she's married. Or was married. I mean for fuck's sake, that's something you'd tell someone."

"We don't know the whole story."

Jamie is quiet. His loyalty lies with Ethan, regardless of who said what to whom, or who did not say what they should have when they had the bloody chance.

"She was good for him. He had a softer side when she was with him – it was nice to see him caring about something other than work and bloody rugby," Fran says.

"And cricket."

"Yes dear, and cricket too."

"And PlayStation Frisbee. Not that he's any good. I totally kick his arse. Tatupu rules!" Jamie raises his arms in victory, the ladder shaking beneath him.

"Watch it!" Fran yelps, feeling spots of sage paint on her head. She stands and stretches her legs. "Time for a break,"

"Time for a Kit Kat," Jamie replies. "Stand back baby, I'm coming down."

"I'm so bloody glad I married you." Fran nuzzles a bit closer to her husband on the laundry door step and rests her head on his shoulder.

"You know," Jamie says, handing his wife her cup of tea, "if you love me that much, you'd better be intending to share that Kit Kat." Liz breaks it in half, and hands the bigger bit over. "You need your energy, Tatupu," she points to the ceiling, "you're painting that next!"

Chapter Twenty-Four

Without logic or reason, at least not any that Lucy is willing to look in to, she does not want a repeat of her night with Tom. *Did I really do that?* Lucy wonders as she scrubs her teeth and stares at herself in the mirror. *Did I really let him do that?*

When she thinks about her night with Tom, she feels a bit like it was someone else. That some other Lucy had spent the night with a stranger.

She has had a brief exchange with Tom.

"Lovely day isn't it?"

"Can I help you with your pack?"

"That would be lovely."

"You are madness," Fritzi announces on the bus ride into Christchurch. "He is going to waste."

"It was a one night thing," Lucy tries to explain.

"If you don't have him, maybe I can?" Fritzi asks as she slicks on a layer of lip gloss and makes kissy fish faces at Lucy.

"He's all yours," Lucy giggles.

"You are good friend," Fritzi says, giving her a hug, and it's only when Lucy sees Fritzi staring intently at Tom, batting her eyelids and flicking her long blonde hair, that Lucy realises she's serious.

For a moment she's annoyed. *I know I don't want him but*

still...

But Lucy looks at them both, at how enthusiastic Fritzi is about Tom's guitar playing skills. *Ah well, what would I have done with him anyway?* Lucy thinks. She zips up her bag, ready to hop off the bus.

Lucy is overcome with an indescribable sadness. They walk through Christchurch, along the safe paths laid through what was once a city, and which now, as if written in some apocalyptic novel, is simply referred to as the red zone. It brings their usually buoyant tour group to an eerie silence as Ben explains about the first earthquake on September 4th, 2010, and the February 22nd, 2011 aftershock, which was even more devastating. The second quake took the lives of a hundred and eighty-five people. They walk silently past bare, stony patches of land, where weeds are taking hold. Past wire fences with flowers and messages left for those who didn't make it home.

Lucy spies a pebble, painted green, with a tiny pink heart carefully painted at its centre. It sits under a canopy of yellow dandelions.

"A hundred and eighty-five hearts, painted on pebbles and stones, scattered round the city in memory of those who died." Ben tells Lucy he had read about them in the newspaper that morning.

They wander around, talking quietly, trying to take in how truly terrifying it must have been. The iconic Christchurch Cathedral lies broken before them, between piles of waist high rubble. *How long will it take them to rebuild their lives?*

Lucy wonders. *Is it even possible?*

A man in a white safety hat wanders over. He's on his lunch break, and between bites of a mince pie and sips from a takeaway coffee, he answers their questions with an open frankness that leaves Lucy in awe of his strength and courage. Surely part of him wanted to tell them to fuck off, that this wasn't a tourist attraction, some freak show to ogle at. But instead he shares with them his history with the street they stand on.

"Over there - that was a coffee shop. They did great sausage rolls." They could see beyond the cordon where the front wall of a café had fallen away, leaving in its place a dusty still-life portrait, coffee cups still on tables, a woman's cardigan slung over the back of the chair. An empty pushchair in a corner.

"Everyone got out," the man says and pats Lucy on the back, seeing her wide eyes focus on the pushchair. Lucy closes her gaping mouth and tries to blink back the tears that threaten.

"Up there," the man continues, "were offices. My uncle was an accountant up there. We'll knock 'em down next week." They all look up at a curtain flapping in the breeze, an exposed desk and chair, a filing cabinet and the phone, still attached at the wall. Lucy almost expected to see someone walk through the door and sit down with their lunch, make a quick phone call or two. She wonders if someone was doing just that when it happened. Just going about their daily life when suddenly the ground was ripped from beneath them and their whole world changed, all in a few seconds.

"I can't run away," the man in the white hat explains, when someone in their group wonders whether it is worth rebuilding, if people will even want to come back. "It's a challenge – a big one – but this is my city. My great-great-granddad was one of the first settlers here. It's who I am and where I belong."

"Didn't you just want to get out?" someone asks.

"Sure," he says, sipping his coffee, contemplating the question. "The aftershocks are pretty full-on sometimes, brings it all back. But I was lucky, my family are all alive. And it helps to be here," he explains. "It might be demolition, but it's good to be doing something, knowing I'm helping get the city ready for its next phase, its new life."

They are quiet once more. "We're determined folk down here," he points out. "It might not happen overnight, but it will happen." He drains his cup of coffee and heads back behind the wire fence.

"Thank you," Lucy calls out, "and I'm sorry for... you know." Lucy shrugs. She wishes she knew what to say. *Sorry for what? Sorry for everything?*

I'm sorry for everything.

The mood on the bus is subdued as they wind their way north, up the east coast of the South Island. Some nap quietly, their iPods bumping gently against their stomachs. Lucy has two seats all to herself. Fritzi had lasted less than half an hour, before wobbling her way up the aisle of the bus to where Tom was sitting. With a wink back to Lucy, she has plonked down beside him, and now Lucy can see their two heads almost touching, deep in conversation that she can't hear and doesn't particularly want to.

He was mine, Lucy thinks, staring out across the rocky shoreline to where she believed the grey sky touched the even greyer ocean. Then she asks herself the question she has been desperately avoiding since she boarded the Zest bus over a month ago.

What am I doing?

Lucy closes her eyes and sees the man with the white safety hat, bulldozing and laying bare his old city, his old life, so that a new one can be built. *My old life is a crumbling mess,* Lucy thinks, *a jumbled twisted mess. Even if I go back, I can only pick up bits of what was once there. It will never be what it was, though it was always a bit of a mishmash of people and places. I know it hasn't always worked very smoothly, but there are things that I hold so dear, people and places that rest so deep within me that I ache to go back and pick them up. To find them and hold them, to hug them, and squeeze so tightly that I might remember them and have them real in my life once more.*

She avoids the photo opportunities on the beach in Kaikoura. The sea is restless, so she turns down a boat ride out to see whales.

With three other stragglers, Lucy decides to stay on the bus, and is rewarded with a free couple of hours in Kekerengu.

The store, a café-slash-restaurant, sits right above the beach, with an open fire glowing warm inside. She chooses a solitary seat beside a window she barely looks at. She tears at a baguette, dipping small pieces into her carrot and kumara soup. She removes her shoes and draws circles with her thick socks on the wooden floor. She closes her eyes and straightens her back, taking a small quiet breath, preparing for the first bar of music, the warmth of the stage lights. She opens her eyes and it's gone. She stirs her spoon slowly in her soup.

How do I do it? Lucy wonders. *How do I clear away the rubble? I can see that the debris from my old life needs to be cleared, but to do that I have to go back.* Lucy isn't sure if she is brave enough. She leaves her soup uneaten and stands outside. She twists her hair into a pony tail, but her curls bounce free in the sea breeze. *I'm tired,* Lucy thinks.

"Aren't you getting tired of running away?" Liz had asked when Lucy called to tell her she was heading off on a tour of New Zealand.

"I'm not running away, I'm finding my own way. Having an adventure. Isn't that what you've been telling me to do?"

"An adventure is a positive life experience Luce," Liz had patiently explained, "How good are you feeling about your life right now?"

"I'm fine," Lucy had answered. "I'm fine."

But I'm not fine, Lucy finally admits, letting silent tears fall unabated. *I ran away, then I ran away again. And I'm not fine.*

Ben looks a bit pissed off when Lucy says she needs her

pack, but there is something very fragile about her, as she tucks her curls behind her ears and bites her lip, hopping from foot to foot impatiently. Her bag is fortunately not too far back, and she thanks him profusely as he lugs it out from under the bus. He watches for a moment as she drags it over to the small grass edge beside the car park, then goes back to his magazine and his spot on the steps of the bus.

    Lucy digs deep inside her pack until her hand connects with the cool plastic and metal of her cell phone. She drags it out, holding it between her teeth as she struggles to zip the rucksack back up, sitting across it and bouncing on top to squish everything down and get the zip done up. She stays straddled on her pack, and stares hard at her phone for a moment. She pushes the power button, waits for the signal and dials his number.

Chapter Twenty-Five

Gilbert Cameron-Jones was simply the most enchanting person Lucy had ever met in all her seventeen years. She first laid eyes on him when she was studying at the English National Ballet School. She was overjoyed to have picked up a couple of roles in *Goldilocks and the Three Bears*, a ballet designed for an audience of young children.

'CJ', as all the fabulously cool people called him, had been signed to the National Ballet two years previously, and his star had shone brightly ever since. Lucy had seen him perform as the Prince in *Sleeping Beauty*, and fallen instantly in love, without ever having spoken a word to him. She was desperate to meet him, so a few months later she had tagged along with a group of field mice from *Cinderella*, who hadn't thought twice about hooking up with the older, more experienced dancers at a local club.

Lucy had barely set foot in her local pub before that, and felt like her underage status was stamped across her forehead for all to see. When she'd seen the bouncer at the door, she'd panicked, desperately fighting the urge to run the other way.

"Come on, sweetheart," CJ had whispered in her ear, hooking his arm through hers, "it'd be a sin not to come in and share those sexy legs of yours." His eyes were a soft brown, almost caramel in colour, and Lucy had found it hard not to stare. He introduced her to James Barrett, one of the ballet's top choreographers, bought her a vodka and lemonade, and regaled her with stories from his own time at ballet school. Some of his stories she'd already heard, folklore being what it was, and Gilbert Cameron-Jones being worthy of a great deal of gossip.

Later that night he had found her a cab, then pulled her close so that, just like a teenage cliché, her knees went weak. His lips grazed her neck and he'd gently pulled her jacket back to kiss her shoulder.

"You're a minx, darling, and if you were a year or two older, I'd take you home and do very bad things to you."

Lucy had never been a girl who attracted attention but, for almost a week, her evening spent beside Gilbert Cameron-Jones had tongues wagging.

The following year Lucy graduated from ballet school, then auditioned and was accepted into the Scottish Ballet for a season of *Desire*. She had auditioned to challenge herself and improve her dancing, not because CJ had the lead. But she watched him in rehearsals, remembering the delicate sensation of his breath on her neck, and she prayed she would not fall on her face when he watched her group taken through their paces.

Desire was a tale of twisted love. War raged in the background as love was found and lost in a crumpled old deserted apartment block on the outskirts of a besieged town. The set was stark and cold, the dancing raw and emotional. Her role as one of a group of prostitutes, credited as 'Ladies of the Night' in the programme, took Lucy right outside her comfort zone. CJ was captivating when he danced, and in her eighteen-year-old world, Lucy stood watching in the wings, then filled her nights with dreams of dancing alongside him.

The first night of *Desire* had been magical, both on and off the stage. Praise flowed from the audience, some of whom were crying, and the jubilant cast had decamped to the pub down the road, a flood of relief replacing first night jitters. Lucy timed it perfectly and arrived at the bar at the same time CJ did.

"The little minx is no longer afraid, I see." His gravelly voice was in her ear again as they slid past the doorman. A whisper of his hand touched her thigh as they squeezed through the crowd to the bar.

"I'm legal now," she'd said, cocking her head to one side and looking up into his brown eyes. "A year or so older." He'd held her gaze for the longest time, then whistled long and low. "You're coming home with me," he'd said, picking up the two drinks he'd paid for and disappearing round the corner of the bar.

Lucy had collected her own drink and gone back to join her fellow dancers. Conversations zigzagged back and forth about the night's performance and who'd been given extra notes, then moved on to the cost of coffee and who knew when the next series of Miranda would be on the telly. Though Lucy's arrival at the table was barely acknowledged, when Gilbert Cameron-Jones appeared at her side and quietly suggested she get her coat, and when she went and did just that, her departure was noted by every single dancer in the room.

He hadn't known he was her first, but he'd burned each touch, each sensation, each moment into Lucy's consciousness. When she retrieved the memory from its small sacred place inside, it could still make her blush furiously, as she had for many nights over the following three months while *Desire* toured the UK.

Lucy and CJ's relationship had developed over the following years, as much as their careers allowed. Stretches of time together were followed by months apart. Then a three year hiatus while CJ danced in Asia. There was no animosity, just a general feeling of being busy following their own careers, and true happiness at being thrown back together after the years apart. Lucy chose not to ask about the in-between times, and she reluctantly realised CJ had little interest in her own comings and goings.

She had met his mother backstage once, but CJ had simply introduced her as his favourite ballerina, something she'd heard him say about others plenty of times before. She heard murmurs, gossip of his conquests, but never found the nerve to bring it up. She longed to sit down and talk with him, to share more, to maybe talk about the future. But something inside told her not to rock the boat. She was grateful for his attention, basking in his confidence and his humour, and when they made love, she felt wanted.

Lucy thought maybe she was in love with him. She

definitely felt lonely when he wasn't around. Their careers still took them in different directions, and their times apart were lengthy –Lucy sometimes wondered if it was worth it. But CJ would reappear, whisk her out to meet fabulous people and hustle her back home, where any thoughts of long-term commitment and settling down were lost in a sea of lust and longing.

That all changed in 2010. Lucy was dancing in *Sleeping Beauty* for the English Ballet and CJ arrived halfway through the season to replace an injured Prince. They had fallen into their usual routine and when the tour ended in May, Lucy found she was exhausted. She felt sluggish in the mornings, and slept more than usual. She was grateful for her inclusion in the low-key children's ballet *Tales of Beatrix Potter*, as it went some way towards taking her mind off the lethargy. She wondered if she was burnt out. She took extra vitamins, went to bed earlier, and started to feel better.

Lucy hadn't had a proper holiday in years and her ankle was causing her a few problems, so after each show she would curl up on the couch with her laptop, and disappear to warmer climates – Australia, Hawaii, the Caribbean. She started to feel excited about the possibility of an extended holiday, a chance to let her body rest.

Her mother called, insisting there was more to life than ballet, and wondering whether Lucy even realised it was summer? On her mother's instructions, Lucy marked on the calendar a barbecue for the following Sunday. As she hung up the phone, she noticed the small *p* in a circle on the previous

Monday's calendar square. She tried desperately to silence the rush of panic.

Wait, wait, she told herself, *hold on, when was it? I've been so bloody busy, was it last month?* She put a hand to her stomach, the same as she had done the day before, insisting to Liz that they had to stop eating so many croissants. Her jeans felt tight where they had once been loose.

She took three tests, then went to the doctor, who confirmed she was pregnant and sent her for a scan. It was her own fault. CJ's surprise arrival had come a couple of weeks before she was due to get her contraceptive injection. Then he'd gone again, so she hadn't bothered. At the scan, a small thing that for twelve weeks had been quietly growing inside her, floated in a bubble on the screen.

"You know I had to ask, darling," CJ had said, and Lucy supposed he was right. But there had been no one else on her part. CJ didn't mention his own faithfulness, or lack thereof. She didn't bother asking.

Each night for the following week, he visited the small flat on Kilburn High Road. Liz would swing open the front door, welcoming CJ, then demanding to know what he'd brought them. CJ had started with chocolate, the bitter, dark variety Lucy pretended to love. A bag of apples was produced next and finally a tub of chocolate ice cream.

"Now we're talking," Lucy had laughed, sticking her finger into the gooey sludge, unwilling to wait for a spoon.

"I've talked to Mother," CJ said, lounging back on the couch.

He'd finished his coffee and was swinging Liz's delicate china cup off his pinkie finger as he spoke.

Put the cup down, Lucy willed him, trying to listen to what he was saying.

"She suggested St Bede's – do it proper next spring. Registry office before then. Baby is a Cameron-Jones so we'll need to be married before he or she pops out."

"Married?" Lucy was trying to catch up. "Us? You want us to get married?"

"Well, don't you?" CJ had looked confused. "We're having a baby. That's the way these things work. We might be a bit arse-about-face, but Mother will thaw out as soon as she's got a grandchild to dress up and parade out at special events. She's been pestering me for a while now."

Married. To CJ. She would have him all to herself. Every day. A family, a home.

"Do you want to? *Really* want to?" Lucy had asked, wanting to be sure.

"Of course," CJ had nodded. The cup continued to swing from his finger.

The following Tuesday, Lucy had woken on her wedding day feeling slightly nauseous and a bit dizzy. She had put it down to marriage jitters and joined Liz, amongst the boxes of her possessions, for a last breakfast together of croissants and cups of tea. The movers would arrive in the next couple of days to shift her into CJ's SW1 apartment – a temporary move until they could find a house to buy.

The registry office had taken less than an hour. CJ's parents had popped in briefly before Mr Cameron-Jones had left for a business lunch and Mrs Cameron-Jones had gone to a dress fitting. Lucy's mother and Liz had come with them to their local pub, where they sipped champagne and ate bangers and mash.

A pain in Lucy's side turned from a niggle to a nightmare, leaving her breathless and hardly able to speak. She stumbled to the bathroom and threw up. Her Mum took one look at her and asked CJ to call an ambulance.

A late-term miscarriage. Lucy held her mother's hand and drifted to sleep. D and C. That's what they had called it. When she opened her eyes, the baby was gone.

CJ brought huge bunches of flowers each time he visited, "They're for my wife," he told the nurses. "Your husband has arrived," he'd say, kissing her on the lips. "I'll find another vase!" His jovial mood wasn't catching. Lucy thought she would rather have a baby than a husband, and then felt wretched and ungrateful for thinking such a thing. He visited before rehearsals each day, but when she was released from hospital, she flew with her mother to Scotland. His week was full, so her mum would look after her while CJ had dress rehearsals and final fittings.

Lucy couldn't remember which ballet it was. *Romeo and Juliet*? Was it something Shakespeare? But then, she didn't really care. She probed her lack of interest briefly, in the gap between *Antiques Roadshow* and Nigella's latest cooking show. But then she got lost in the chocolate fudge sauce. She phoned her mum to pick up ice cream on the way home.

CJ came at the weekend but, where Lucy found the peace of the countryside calmed her soul, CJ was anxious and edgy, unable to sit still. He went to the local pub, rolled home at closing with tales of a man who played pool for Ireland. Or maybe it was polo.

"Is he always like this?" her mum had asked.

"I think so," Lucy replied, but she didn't really know.

A week later, she returned to London, to CJ's city apartment, where the doorman welcomed her as Mrs Cameron-Jones. Her boxes were stacked against a wall in the spare room. CJ hadn't thought to even unpack her clothes.

She wandered aimlessly with a cup of tea, slightly frightened by the very masculine leather furniture and the clean, stark surfaces. She'd never really noticed how tidy he was before. She thought perhaps she'd have a lie down, but was waylaid by the slim laptop on the side table. She hadn't checked her emails in over a week.

She sat on the side of the bed and powered it up. Skype blinked and pinged. CJ was still signed in with his own account. Lucy was snooping. And the reward was a conversation she was never meant to see.

Call me before your little wifey comes home. If I'm to be your scarlet woman, I feel it's important I dress for the part. I've a little racy lacy number for your eyes only, Mr Cameron-Jones!

Leaving now – be there by noon.

Lucy lay on the bed staring at the ceiling. She pondered how peculiar it was that her husband was out consummating their marriage with someone else. She felt cold, but couldn't be bothered to lift the blankets. She thought of the places she had googled just a few weeks ago and longed for the feeling of sunshine and warmth on her skin.

She should have been angry and a small part of her was, but she found she was too tired to do as Liz suggested and scrub the toilet with his toothbrush. She found the number of the company she had used to move her things to CJ's apartment, and paid fifty extra pounds to have them move them back to Liz's that afternoon.

"My mother is going to be a handful," CJ said, "not that you need to worry about that." They were in the sitting room, waiting for the doorman to call up to let her know her taxi had arrived. He patted her knee and kissed her head.

"Will you be okay?"

"Absolutely," Lucy nodded, "it's for the best, really."

"Probably," CJ nodded. "I'll sort the lawyers – you don't need to worry about a thing."

And so Lucy hadn't. She had gone back to Liz's, where she had changed into her pyjamas and found herself physically unable to do anything more than eat jam toast and sob salty tears at the emptiness that raged inside. She had lost a baby and a husband in the space of two weeks, though the first she had hardly had time to connect with, and the second she was quite sure she didn't want anyway. It was all so complicated and messy, and her brain wouldn't function to sort it all out.

"Hormones," her mother explained. "Give it another week or so, I know it's a blasted pain, but give it time."

And eventually Lucy started to feel somewhat normal again. She volunteered at a local ballet school for a term, loving her time with the little ones in their tiny pink leotards with their eager faces. She was offered a small role by a friend of a friend of CJ's, but she knew he was calling in a favour, and she found herself with no desire to put herself through another gruelling tour.

"I'm going to say no," she told Liz. They were watching *QI*, eating bread and butter pudding. "I'm going to New Zealand."

"On your way to Timbuktu?" Liz had laughed.

"No really, I'm going to New Zealand. Home. I was born there, remember? It's where my dad is."

"I thought he wasn't much of a show in the fathering department?" Liz said, scraping her spoon in the bowl to get the last of the custard.

"He's always sent money," Lucy said. "It would be nice to see him in the flesh. And I need a holiday."

"You do need a holiday," Liz agreed, "an adventure!"

"What better place to start than the other side of the world?" Lucy smiled, the excitement bubbling inside, a smile stretching across her face.

"Do it!" Liz had demanded. So she had.

Chapter Twenty-Six

"About bloody time you returned to civilisation. Where on earth are you?"

Lucy smiles at the familiar voice and feels a touch of longing for her old life.

"Top of the South Island," she tells him, but CJ's not listening – instead he's talking to someone else in the room.

"I'm on the phone to my wife, I'll be with you in a minute."

"But Liz said the annulment came through," Lucy yells into her cell phone. She'll kill him if it hasn't.

"Sorry, beautiful. *Ex*-wife," he clarifies to whoever he is sharing the room with. "I did leave a message. I got a number from your mum, spoke to some bloke. Evan? He said you were on a bus in the middle of nowhere."

Ethan knows where I am. Lucy tries to ignore the rush of heat she feels at hearing his name.

"What did Ethan say?"

"Who?"

"The bloke."

"What bloke?"

Lucy holds the phone in front of her and rolls her eyes.

"The one you spoke to. What did he say?"

"Not a lot, actually, bit of a moody prick. Said you'd moved on, off on a tourist bus or something. Aren't they for nineteen-year-olds in their gap years, who want nothing more than to drink and hump?"

"It's been great actually – I've been bungy jumping and riding horses."

"Is that a euphemism, darling? I have heard those Antipodeans are well-hung," CJ laughs loudly. "I bet you're having a ball!"

Lucy sighs.

"Yes, Ethan, I'm having a ball, it's all big willies and shagging around the clock." Ben looks up from his magazine and gives Lucy a wink.

"CJ."

"What?"

"Darling, you just called me Ethan."

"I didn't."

"You did."

"I didn't call you Ethan," Lucy says firmly.

"You did." Ben looks up briefly from his magazine and mouths at her 'you said Ethan'. He shrugs at the look of thunder Lucy throws his way and quickly puts his head back down.

"Anyway, darling, I suppose you'll be after written proof of our divorce."

"Annulment."

"*Potayto, potahto*," CJ laughs. "I've sent a copy to your mother, but if you like I can scan my copy and email it to you."

"No, no, it's fine." Lucy sighs. She sits down on the grass, stretches out and stares up at the clouds merging and turning in the sky above her head.

"You know, I was just thinking, we never talked much... about anything." Lucy says.

"We were far too busy doing unspeakable things," CJ laughs. "Do you know they gave the Frog Prince to Rufus? Honestly, darling, he's like a baby elephant up there."

Why did I call? Lucy asks herself. *I wanted to talk about us, about our baby, our marriage, our annulment.* But now that she has him on the line, Lucy finds herself rather anxious to hang up.

"Are you still there?" CJ asks. "This time delay does my head in, darling – it's like you're calling from the afterlife."

"I'm here," Lucy replies. *But I'm not there. Not anymore. Not in the afterlife, but in life after CJ.* And life after Ethan. The first Lucy is very relieved about, the second she doesn't much want to think about.

"Thanks, CJ, for doing the paperwork. And I'm sorry, about the whole... you know..."

"No apologies," CJ replies firmly. "We were fabulous, Lucy – it was great fun. I save my regrets for the things I haven't done."

"Your philosophy on life?" Lucy enquires.

"It's on the poster hanging on the wall here in front of me," CJ laughs. "See you later darling, mind those Aussies, and whatever they tell you, don't eat the Vegemate."

"Kiwis. And Vege*mite*." Lucy says. But the line is dead.

The bus ride from Kaikoura is a bit of a blur. At Seddon

they make a toilet stop. The wind has settled and the sky has taken on a pink hue in the late afternoon. Lucy feels cold, and she shivers beneath her puffer jacket while she waits in the queue. They board the bus once more, and curl around the coastal road.

They drive through a small seaside town, and Lucy looks for signs of life on the main street as they trundle by. But it's after four-thirty in the afternoon and the bookshop, the café and what looks like a small antiques store all have 'closed' signs hanging from their doors.

They turn off the sealed road and the bus crunches through gravel, the passengers marvelling at the endless rows of perfectly spaced grapevines, dipping and rising across the hills in undulating waves.

Gilchrist Point Wines has barrack-style accommodation in a brand new barn, a stone's throw from the vineyard. The inside is fitted with bunk beds and camp style bathrooms. It is perfect for capturing a few tourist dollars, and a very clever marketing tool for a comparatively young company trying to get a foothold in a very tough market. Lucy knows she should be admiring the beautiful brick fireplace and soaking in the view out across the Pacific Ocean from the main reception area. But she is tired. And grumpy. She forgoes the free platters of fruit and crackers provided and makes for the barn, where she picks a corner bunk. Then, taking her towel and her toilet bag, she wallows under a long, hot shower.

Dinner is a magnificent affair and, with a glass of Gilchrist

Pinot in hand, Lucy's mood begins to mellow. Amongst the grapevines a long row of tables is pushed together. Red and white chequered tablecloths dance in the evening breeze and outdoor gas heaters are dotted down the rows to keep away the chill. Many of Lucy's group have already taken rough woollen blankets from the pile stacked haphazardly in a wheelbarrow at one end of the table and draped them over their shoulders and legs for an extra layer of warmth.

Garlic bread drips with butter and olive oil, the chicken ravioli is a dream with its zing of lemon and hit of parsley and thyme. The wine flows and Lucy keeps her glass topped up. She listens hard to the conversations around her. Germany bailing out Greece... the Euro in crisis... what is the difference between a cupcake and a muffin? Is there anyone keen to visit Brazil in the next few months? *I'm here, in the now,* Lucy decides. *I'm not going to think about anything else.*

She admires her motley crew of fellow travellers. She is happy to dawdle at the back of the pack, being led down the garden path by Ben and the guy who owns the vineyard. Or perhaps he is the manager. Is his father the owner? He was introduced earlier, but Lucy can't remember his name.

"I shall call him Wine Man," she tells no one in particular, and a crooked grin spreads across her face as she tries to concentrate on the zigzagging path that leads them down to the beach. Lucy trips on a tree root but manages to catch her balance. She rests, bent over, hands on her knees, and shakes her head at the small, innocuous root, then jogs to catch up with the others who are almost on the beach.

There is a campfire roaring, and they all sit down around it. Lucy finds a sandy spot and watches across the fire as Wine Man pulls a large wheel of Camembert from a flax basket. Ben strums his guitar, and while the cheese is held over the fire, Lucy listens to Wine Man talk about the lighthouse on the hill behind them. He talks of the rough coastline, and the eighteen shipwrecks between 1845 and 1947.

"Gilchrist Point Lighthouse was built in 1871," he tells them. "It was a wooden construction which, within ten years, began rotting away in the harsh, exposed conditions. Winters here bring driving rain and the corrosive sand whips up in the wind. They say the old lighthouse whistled and creaked and groaned like an old man whenever its lighthouse keeper attempted to open the doors or climb its stairs."

Lucy watches as Wine Man holds the large white cheese over the flames, tossing sand over the edges of the fire to cool the heat. His rhapsodic tone pulls the group in and holds them captive.

He talks of an old lighthouse keeper, James someone, whose resourcefulness gained him a pile of bricks from up north, a hand-drawn diagram and written instructions from America, and a local community willing to pitch in.

"The brick lighthouse behind you became operational on March 7th, 1907, when the oil-burning lamp was transferred from the old rickety wooden lighthouse to its new, sturdy brick home."

Lucy lies back in the sand and stares up at the lighthouse.

"It used to be taller," Wine Man tells the group, "but a big storm some time during the Second World War knocked the lantern clean off. A lightning strike, they say. By then they had the lighthouse at Cape Campbell, and Gilchrist was decommissioned."

Lucy and her fellow travellers take pieces of baguette as it's handed around.

"Hard lives," Wine Man continues. "Long, lonely nights, harsh conditions – especially hard on families. They used to move the keepers and their families around, so their time at the more isolated stations, such as Puysegur Point in the far south and Cuvier Island up north, was balanced with stations like Point Gilchrist, with its village nearby.

Lucy stares into the night. Somewhere out there, on the other side of the ocean, is the North Island. Wellington. Island Bay. The little house on the hill, *Top Gear* on the telly, tea and biscuits. Georgie. And Ethan. It feels light years away. Lucy closes her eyes and thinks of Pencarrow Lighthouse at Eastbourne. In her mind, she retraces the distance she walked with Ethan to reach it. She remembers the little white fence around the grave of a small child and wonders about how the child's mother coped with her loss. *Was she lonely?* Lucy wonders. *Did she look at that little grave each day and wonder why? Aren't lighthouses supposed to save lives?* Lucy thinks, and mulls over this contradiction in her head.

Lucy will always remember waking up in that hospital bed, a hollow, raw feeling where a life had once been. She clenches her stomach and grabs a fistful of sand. A moment later she loosens her grip and lets it slip through her hand.

Everyone said how brave she was, but Lucy isn't so sure about that.

I had a doctor and nurses and medicine. Those lighthouse keepers' wives were alone. Who helped them when they had their babies? Who held their hands when those babies died? Lucy thinks that's true strength and bravery. *Each storm that struck, they had no choice but to hunker down and survive.*

Isn't that what I did? I survived, didn't I? Yes, but those women lived in isolation, and yet they stood alongside their husbands and saved more lives, more souls than they probably would have even met in their lifetimes. They were all alone, and yet they were the light that shone through the dark, guiding ships to safety through the rough waves and stormy seas. I was never alone. I had CJ, for what he was worth, and when I didn't think I could face another day, I had Mum and Liz. I doubt I would have survived my storm without them. And when the sky cleared and the seas calmed, and I had the strength to step out of the dark, well, that's when I found Ethan.

Wine Man slices gooey wedges from the wheel and squashes the cheese onto their hunks of bread, drawing his guests in close to him. But Lucy can't move. In the warmth of the fire, she drops her head.

"I miss Ethan," Lucy whispers, remembering his sandy hair blowing in the breeze, his hand around hers. The way he had spent forever with his head tilted to the left, his chin raised slightly, lost in the shape and structure of the lighthouse at Pencarrow. She could have spent forever alongside him.

Lucy's hair falls across her face in a curtain of curls, while salty tears make the uneaten bread soggy in her hands. She is quiet and still.

Fritzi and Tom find Lucy, struggling for breath between silent sobs. Fritzi shoves the last of her cheesy bread in her mouth and swallows hard. Using gentle fingers she separates the curls covering Lucy's face and kisses her forehead.

"You are needing to talk," she says. It is not a question, rather a direction. "You will take some breaths and I will wait till you are able. Go away, Tom. There is coffee in the urns. You will make some with sugar." Tom does as he is told.

"I miss him," Lucy sobs. "I don't know what I'm doing."

"Oh dear," Fritzi says.

"I had a baby. A miscarriage. It was hellish. I thought I loved CJ, but I didn't. I love Ethan. Ethan would love this. He took me to a lighthouse once. He knows all about them."

Fritzi sits close to Lucy and rubs her back. She listens as Lucy talks about the tall, good-looking man who is going to Dubai because Lucy lied.

"Well, I didn't lie, but I didn't tell the truth," she explains as a loud sob escapes and a fresh batch of tears falls. "But it's all the same thing."

At Fritzi's insistence, Lucy goes back to the beginning and explains about CJ and the baby she lost at fifteen weeks, and about Ethan, the man who filled her with such love and laughter. She talks about how she has ended up on this beach, at the bottom of the world, as far away from all her problems as she can physically get.

Tom returns with coffee and they sit quietly until Lucy talks again – this time about Sharon, with her big boobs and her shiny hair. How she had blown in, claiming Ethan for her own.

"Bitch," Tom says, "I know the type," then he goes back to drinking his coffee.

"But I had a husband, and I didn't tell him. Why didn't I tell him?" Lucy asks, and Fritzi hugs her tightly.

"What a mess," Lucy attempts to laugh, wiping tears on her sleeve. They sit quietly again, listening to a small group singing *Ten Guitars* on the other side of the camp fire.

"I have to get over it. Over it all," Lucy explains. "I need to draw a line in the sand," she says and, picking up a small piece of driftwood, she does just that. "A line between my old life and whatever my new life is going to be. It's just that I'm not sure what that is, yet."

"Maybe you can't." Fritzi says. "You want to make the two lives, but maybe that is small bit greedy. One life, Lucy," she insists, taking her hand and squeezing it hard. "One life that is messy, and annoying, and dirty and hard. And happy and joyful and fun, and sad and heart-breaking. But it's yours. Not all perfect. You're not perfect person. Who is? You have pain, yes, but not so you are special. Everyone else has hard time, too." Fritzi nods her head firmly and squeezes Lucy's hand again.

"But I messed it all up," Lucy groans. "It's just not worked out the way I thought it would."

"I steal pair of shoes when I am fourteen," Fritzi says. "Okay, I steal lots of pair of shoes. My mother, she work in the shop. I am shameful to her. I have to clean the shop toilets and floors for a whole year for punishment. Otherwise, manager will call police and I am going to prison."

"And I have a son," Tom says, reaching into his pocket and pulling out a picture of a little boy on a tricycle. "He's three, now. I see him once a month and on his birthday and Christmas. He's adopted. His parents are great. I was only seventeen," he shrugs. "Now that was messed up."

"I had girlfriend back home," Fritzi says, "but now I like the boy." She smiles at Tom, whose eyes are almost popping out of his head.

"Let's talk about that!" Tom demands, and Lucy laughs.

"Not now, Tom, now we are talking to Lucy," Fritzi says firmly. "You are not needing two lives. One life is fine. Is good, you live with what you have."

One life, Lucy thinks.

"But how can I live with all this mess?" Lucy asks.

"But it's *your* mess," Fritzi explains, "not supposed to be tidy lines. Is like a map of your life so far. Lots of different roads!"

"And right now the map is wide open," Tom puts in.

"You can follow new path," Fritzi says, "wherever you are wanting to go."

"I'm tired," Lucy yawns. "What if I don't want to go anywhere?"

"Then don't," Fritzi says. "Choice is all yours!"

Chapter Twenty-Seven

Lucy wakes early the next morning. Her face feels tight and her nose is still blocked from the tears she went to sleep with. She slides quietly from her bunk bed and pulls on her jeans. She stuffs her curls into a ponytail and carries her jacket and shoes to the door, sliding it quietly open. She sits to tie her laces on the outside step.

"First up, eh?" Wine Man is pushing a wheelbarrow full of potatoes. His large rubber gumboots slap against his shins as he walks and crunch on the gravel underfoot. "Coffee's just brewing in the kitchen."

"Thanks," Lucy replies. "I think I'll have a wee walk first."

The man stops pushing and points up a path.

"Take a left just up over the rise – it's only a few minutes' walk to the lighthouse."

"Thanks," Lucy says, and goes back to tying her laces while Wine Man goes back to his wheelbarrow of potatoes.

The path is little more than a beaten track through the seagrass. The sun is a while away from rising and Lucy tugs her jacket tight against the cool sea breeze. She sucks in lungfuls of salty air and concentrates on where she is putting her feet in the dim pre-dawn light. The path is sandy and stony so she keeps her eyes down, planning each footstep. She stops every now and then to gaze out across the South Pacific Ocean, its vast grey surface broken only by the distant skyline.

A few minutes on, as Wine Man had said, the sandy path slopes into a semi-circle of grass and there, hidden behind a retaining wall, is a garden of flowers so perfectly cared for that Lucy can't see a single weed amongst the pansies, the primulas and the few early crocuses that are dotted between the pale pink carnations. A small cottage sits quietly under the lighthouse standing guard on the cliff just above it. There are a pair of gumboots on the backdoor step and a box of slug pellets. Lucy turns her gaze upward. She can feel the lighthouse watching over her. Its thick white cylinder and glass dome demand attention, and reward her reverence with a bright shot of light as the sun reaches over the horizon, its beams hitting the glass and reflecting back out across the ocean.

It is tempting to seek out the warmth of the sun, but Lucy decides to stay in the shady garden for a moment. She takes in the hardy winter flowers and smiles widely at the sight of two garden gnomes, her pink gown joined forever to his blue belted pant suit, their ceramic bodies swaying gently in the breeze, tied as they are with an old rope to the branch of a pohutukawa tree that hovers protectively over the garden.

"Gnomeo and Juliet," a woman's voice calls. Lucy jumps and her hand flies to her chest.

"Good lord," she exclaims, catching her breath.

"Afraid not," the woman says, "but he was here last week – helped me prune the roses." Lucy watches the woman as she slides her feet into the gumboots on the back doorstep of the cottage and shuffles down the steps. She moves slowly across the grass until she is right by Lucy's side.

"Arthritis in me knees," she announces. "I'm to have an operation." Her thick pink dressing gown is tied tightly round her middle, and she pulls from her pocket a grey and white knitted beanie with a pompom on the top.

"Ouch," Lucy sympathises, "but my friend Liz, her Aunty Louise back home had it done and afterwards she said she felt like a teenager again."

"I should have had them done already," the woman says, leaning over and giving the gnomes a gentle push so they rock back and forth, the girl gnome's cheeks flushed red, the boy's smile wide.

"Gnomeo and Juliet," the woman says again.

"Like the movie?" Lucy asks.

"Eh?" the woman replies. "Bloody ridiculous things, but what can I do with 'em? Can't take 'em down. Robert would have me guts for garters. You know he wanted one of them peein' statues out the front. Silly old fool." She shuffles around to where the yellow roses are still sleeping quietly, their buds closed tight. "Charlotte," she says, turning a bud over in her hand, then doing the same with a leaf.

"Lucy," Lucy says, taking in the pompom on Charlotte's hat and wondering if she might be a sandwich or two short of a picnic. "I'm staying at the vineyard."

"That's nice, dear," the woman replies. "You'll see Charlotte as soon as that sun gets a move on. Beautiful blooms, and the smell is incredible. My daughter is named after this rose."

The picnic basket is fully stocked, Lucy realises.

"Does your husband... Robert? Does he help with the garden?" Lucy asks, feeling she should probably add something to the conversation, but not knowing anything about roses.

"Robert? Oh no dear, he's dead." the woman says. "No need for the appalled look, how were you to know? Anyway, three years ago now. The cancer. Came on slowly and dragged on for so long we were both glad for it in the end. Not that I don't miss him every day, but I'll be with him again eventually."

Lucy nods.

"Mabel. That's me," the woman takes a leathered hand from her dressing gown pocket and holds it out for Lucy to shake.

"I'm Lucy, from the vineyard," Lucy says again, "I'm on the Zest Bus," she explains.

"A backpacker, eh?" Mabel nods. "Are you having a good time?"

"I am," Lucy smiles, "at least I have had. Three weeks I've been going, and the others are a bit younger than I am. I'll admit to feeling a bit jaded now."

"Cup of tea?" Mabel asks, and Lucy accepts, but prays a little bit that Mabel might have a proper teapot and cups with saucers, as they go up the back stairs into Mabel's house.

"Keep your jacket on a minute," Mabel directs Lucy, "the fire takes a while to get going." Lucy does as she is told and, as Mabel puts the kettle on and fusses about in her pantry, Lucy takes in the well-worn rug, the floral couch and the small television. An oversized wicker basket holds a selection of brightly coloured wools and what looks like the head of a snowman, complete with straw hat and carrot nose.

"The toys are for the grandchildren," Mabel calls, "I've done a clown and a Scottish piper too."

"They're fabulous!" Lucy says, "I've always wanted to knit."

"I only started after Robert died," Mabel says, taking the lid off a floral teapot that matches the couch perfectly and putting a bunch of tea bags inside.

"I don't do loose leaf," Mabel speaks into the pantry, "all that faffing about. You want it loose, you go and see Mrs Burrows!"

"Mrs Burrows?" Lucy asks, holding a frame and smiling at the faded photo of Mabel and a man who she guesses is Robert. They are wearing matching floral bathers, and smiling brightly at the photographer, squashed up together on an orange sun lounger.

"She runs The Lonely Jandal," Mabel says, "café back in the village. Best ginger crunch you'll ever have."

"Yoyo biscuits?" Lucy asks. "They're my favourite."

"You ask her, she'll make 'em. Now come and have your tea."

Mugs of tea are accompanied by thick slices of bread, browned under the grill and topped with thick slabs of cold butter and boysenberry jam.

"Just like *Milly Molly Mandy*," Lucy smiles.

"The bread an' the jam are both homemade. There's half a dozen boysenberry plants in the back garden," Mabel explains, "too many to keep up with nowadays."

"I can make jam," Lucy says, trying not to speak with her mouth full, but unwilling to wait to start the next bite, "but this is heaven in a jar."

Lucy finishes two cups of tea from her mug. It might not be a cup and saucer, but it does have the faces of Prince William and his new wife Kate on it. She is quietly chuffed. She polishes off three slices of toast, and Mabel indicates she's quite satisfied with that.

Mabel thinks Lucy's eyes look less puffy, her somewhat washed-out complexion a happier shade of peachy pink, and so she sets about getting the dishes done.

"You wash, I'll dry, since you don't know where things go. Then you'll give me a minute to get dressed and I'll show you the lighthouse."

The dirt path leads past the boysenberry plants, through a squeaky gate and up the hill to where the wind whips Lucy's hair as it has before, standing under a different lighthouse. Lucy ponders how a few months can feel like a lifetime. She stands side by side with Mabel in the now bright sunshine, their chins raised and eyes shaded with their hands.

"It's short," Lucy says, thinking back to Pencarrow.

"Big storm in 1952. Its top caved in. Some of the old folk from the village might tell you it was struck by lightning, but they just don't want to admit it was built wrong. The first time I stood here with my Robert, it was just a stunted chimney and a pile of bricks.

'Mabel,' he said, 'I can fix this.' So he went and saw the farmer and he got a good price for the land, and he did fix it.

That's as high as he got when we learned about the cancer. So he put the top on and that's just how it is."

"I like it," Lucy said, pressing her hands against its cool white wall and stretching her arms out as if to engulf the structure in a big hug.

"Grand plans," Mabel dug her hand deep into her polar fleece jacket and produced a heavy black key. "Robert thought he'd like us to live in here eventually, but the cottage is cosy and easy to heat. Imagine the power bill in a place like this!"

Lucy steps inside the lighthouse. It is a huge empty vessel, its whitewashed walls a blank canvas.

"Supposed to be a staircase there." Mabel points upwards, and Lucy follows her arm to where light from the thick panes of stained glass above them shines in sunbeams, crossing over each other in a rainbow of colours.

"It's beautiful," Lucy smiles, "perfect."

"It's a wee bit special," Mabel nods.

"I wish he was here." Lucy whispers.

"So do I, sugar, so do I."

"I'll be sad to go," Mabel says, turning the heavy black key in the lock and putting it back in her fleece pocket. "But in all honesty, it was Robert's dream, and though I've been happy to share it, I've a few things I'd like to do for myself once I get the dodgy knees sorted out."

"When will you be moving?" Lucy asks, following after Mabel as she slowly and carefully shuffles down the path.

"Mrs Burrows's son is in the real estate business, back in

Blenheim. She said he'd come and take a look as soon as I'm ready. I thought I'd get him to do it while I'm away in Wellington having the surgery. I don't need to see strangers traipsing through my cottage, talking about knocking out walls and adding an annex, or one of them awful aluminium conservatories. Do you watch the Living Channel?" Mabel asks Lucy. "Terrible what they do to some of those old buildings." The two women shuffle on, past the cottage, across the pea gravel on the driveway, back to the garden where Gnomeo and Juliet are still swinging gently under the old pohutukawa tree.

"See," Mabel says, beckoning Lucy to come and smell a large yellow blossom. "Charlotte. Isn't she beautiful?"

Lucy thanks Mabel for her kindness, for the tea and the toast and especially the lighthouse. And Robert – for sharing Robert.

On the one hand, Lucy knows she should get a move on, or she'll miss the bus to the next stop. But on the other hand, Lucy knows she would not be so bothered if she arrived to find they had left without her. Fritzi would miss her, but then Fritzi had Tom. *I felt calm. In the garden, in the cottage. I want to go back and hug the lighthouse again. I want to feel its cool exterior on my cheek and soak up its strength.*

But Lucy has signed up for the sea kayaking this afternoon. She quickens her pace. She is about three quarters of the way back to the vineyard when she thinks, *If I wasn't going kayaking, what else would I do? Hang about here? Buy a lighthouse?*

I'd buy a lighthouse.

Lucy turns and runs. Her heart is beating with an urgency she doesn't ever remember feeling before.

"I know what I want, I know what I want," she chants as she trips on the root of a tree, stumbling into the dirt, but picks herself up and runs on.

"Mabel," Lucy calls, banging on the front door of the cottage. "Mabel, are you there?" Lucy can hear the crinkle of a newspaper, the shuffle of slippers on the stone floor, and finally the creak as the heavy door swings open.

"Good heavens," Mabel says, "you look like you've been dragged through the boysenberry bushes backwards. Has old Jim's pig escaped again? Big black thing, he does like to chase the folks from out of town. He wouldn't hurt you, mind, though given a chance he'd probably lick you to death."

"Mabel," Lucy pants, "I'll buy it. The lighthouse. The cottage. I'll buy it."

"But you're a backpacker!" Mabel says, ushering Lucy in and sitting her at the old wooden table.

"I've got money," Lucy claims, and while Mabel dabs Dettol onto the scrapes on the palms of her hands, Lucy explains about her mother and her father and the money that's never been spent. Lucy gets the number from Mabel and calls the vineyard. She tells Ben to drive on without her, and asks him to please tell Fritzi that Lucy will text her soon.

Mabel boils the kettle and produces a tin of shortbread.

"I've a price in mind," Mabel says. "I'll not be a walkover."

Lucy nods, "Absolutely!"

"There's a new townhouse development down by the harbour in Wellington. One bedroom, fully carpeted, and a spa bath, would you believe! And I'll need enough for the cruise. Willie and Wendy – they have the orchard on the other side of town – well, they did a cruise a couple of years ago and all the food was included in the price. Wendy said you can have three desserts if you want to!"

Lucy holds her hot mug of tea with her fingertips so as not to hurt the graze on the palm of her hand.

"We'd have to do it all proper," Mabel warns, giving Lucy a long hard stare. "This is all a bit sudden, for both of us. I think it best if you stay for a week or so. Get to know the area. Then if you're still interested, I'll get Jim round and we can talk turkey."

"Jim with the pigs?" Lucy asks, wanting very much to meet Jim, and Mrs Burrows from the café, and Wendy and Willie who own the orchard.

"That's him. He's also a lawyer." Mabel breaks her shortbread in two pieces. "Most people round here have more than one job. Charlotte tells me in the city they call it multi-tasking, but round here we call it getting on with things."

Lucy smiles and slurps her tea. *It's time to get on with things.*

Chapter Twenty-Eight

Ethan changes his Facebook status to show his new location.

He has been through a rigorous orientation, received fifty emails by his second morning on the job, and has more deadlines than will fit on his calendar. His ear is permanently attached to his cell phone. He has people calling him constantly, wanting yes or no answers, and they then go and do the opposite of what he has told them. Then call him back to complain.

"That's not what I said," is a line he repeats a lot in his first month on the job.

"I told you that wouldn't work. That's not what I said to do." He can't understand why they don't listen. He wonders what the problem is.

Benjamin Braunstein, the tall thin American with the job title of "Communications Facilitator," had called Ethan into his large corner office. Over coffee and muffins, he explained the 'situation'.

"At Aquiro, there are no problems. Only 'situations', that it's your job to 'handle'. No one cares who said what to whom or when. What the client wants, no, *needs,* are results." If Ethan has a situation, it is Ethan who must find a solution.

Braunstein was careful and polite, but when Ethan left his office, he was under no illusions that he was being told to suck it up. Solve problems, get results. That was what he was being paid for.

So Ethan arrives at his desk before seven each morning, and leaves after nine most nights.

"I'll fix that," becomes his new mantra, his work ethic. His popularity rises overnight. Clients thank him for his dedication, for taking their calls after hours, for always being available.

Braunstein takes him for drinks, and asks him to join his family for Thanksgiving. And though it is forty degrees outside, Ethan eats turkey and yams and sweet potato pie. He plays football in the swimming pool with Braunstein's sons. He discusses projects over coffee and cake in 'the den', and as a reward for his hard work, Ethan is added to another committee on another project.

On Sundays Ethan rests. He wakes up late and eats breakfast in the small deli below his apartment where the coffee is rich and strong, giving him the energy he needs to work his way through the tourist activities in his *Lonely Planet* guide. He tells himself he is enjoying the experiences, rather than simply furnishing his Facebook profile with information and photos so that his friends can 'like' them and tell him how jealous they are of his flashy new lifestyle.

He doesn't see Sharon. She leaves messages each time she flies into Dubai. Leaves the names of random bars and clubs, hotels and room numbers where he might find her, should he feel like it. He never does.

He plays squash with a couple of the guys from Finance,

and Lisa and Fay from reception take him to the gold souk, where they help choose the perfect pair of earrings for him to send home to his mum. They all get drunk and sing karaoke and, back at his apartment, he makes them cups of tea and toast. Ethan sleeps on the couch so they can have his bed, though Lisa would happily kick Fay to the couch, for a night under the covers with a sexy Kiwi bloke.

But he doesn't seem attracted to either girl, and they giggle under the duvet, wondering if he might be gay, or perhaps that woman Georgie he got the necklace for is more than just a friend.

Ethan tries not to think too much about home, and on the nights he can't sleep, he drinks a single shot of malt whiskey and watches Formula One or NASCAR until he falls asleep in the ergonomic La-Z-Boy that came with his fully-furnished apartment.

"I'm living the dream," he tells Georgie when she phones. "It's thirty-seven degrees here today. What's it like in Wellington?"

"Fuck off!" Georgie replies, "Eight degrees and southerly."

"See," Ethan says. "Why would I consider coming back to that?"

"Have you," Georgie asks, "considered coming back?"

"I've only been gone four months."

"Homesick? Missing me terribly, aren't you?"

"Like a hole in the head," Ethan laughs.

But Ethan knows he isn't homesick, for the empty feeling is the same one that had been there at home in New Zealand, the same one that has followed him to Dubai. It no longer overwhelms him, as it had in the first few weeks. He is a success at work, he has made good friends and is banking more money than he had ever imagined. So what if there were moments when he feels such an intense need to hear Lucy's voice that he sits in his chair holding his cell phone, hovering over her phone number, but unable to press the call button.

So what if there are times he stares into the mirror while brushing his teeth, lost in memories of her singing in the shower, talking and laughing over the steam.

Does it mean anything that he still buys Jaffa Cakes? Ethan decides that none of it really matters. *This is my life,* Ethan thinks, *I'm out here, doing what I've always wanted to do.*

I'm climbing the ladder, Ethan tells himself.

But what's at the top?

Chapter Twenty-Nine

Lucy is in love. In ten days, her impulsive decision to stay has given her the time and space she had not known she was missing.

Mabel is used to bustling about uninterrupted, and so Lucy has found herself with hours to spare. She has walked the beach, conversing with the gulls and letting the sea spray wrap her in its icy mist. And when the rain swooped in, turning Gilchrist damp and dull, Lucy took a sleeping bag and a thermos and holed up inside the lighthouse for a whole day, reading old Sweet Valley High novels that had once belonged to Mabel's daughter Charlotte.

In the evenings, Lucy is a willing sous chef, letting Mabel boss her about the place, peeling carrots, dicing onions and setting the table with the floral tablecloth and the salt and pepper shakers that look like little kiwis.

The fire is warm and when Mabel goes to bed, Lucy sits and thinks. She cries for the baby she never knew, acknowledges the ridiculous amount of time she spent waiting around for CJ, a man she never really knew, and tries to quell the fear that she has let the very real love she had with Ethan slip away.

But each morning she walks up the path to the lighthouse. She stretches her arms around the curve of the whitewashed walls and feels safe and calm. She knows she is exactly where she needs to be.

Lucy puts aside an afternoon for re-connecting. She starts with the easy phone calls. She speaks to her mum, who is truly delighted to hear her daughter's voice, if a little confused about her desire to buy a lighthouse.

"It's a big responsibility," she says, and Lucy agrees, and promises she is thinking seriously before she signs anything. No, she has not been offered any drugs and no, she would not take them even if she was.

Next she calls Fritzi, who has decided Tom is:

"The big one, the big lover of my life, wink wink, you know what I am talking about, yes Lucy?" and Fritzi roars with laughter.

Calling Georgie takes nerves of steel. Lucy has considered that perhaps the connection between herself and Georgie was Ethan, and now he is gone, there might be nothing left.

"Say you're sorry for running away and not calling or texting and that you will never do it again," Georgie demands.

"I'm sorry," Lucy whispers, I promise I'll never do it again."

"Good," Georgie says. She tells Lucy that Chris is a nightmare to live with; he spends more time in the kitchen than Nigella-bloody-Lawson, and he won't let her drive his car.

"Now tell me all about your bus thingie," Georgie demands, and so Lucy starts with seeing the bus at the library, and ends with the lighthouse above her. Does Georgie think she should?

"Am I mad?" she asks.

"Don't be a chicken." Georgie says. "Do it!"

Mabel and Lucy are sitting on wooden stools in Jim's kitchen. He slides mugs of tea across the orange bench top.

"It's a 1960s original," Jim brags, rubbing his hand across the surface of the bench. "Found it on the side of the road in Picton. I was just driving past, and it was lying there. The owner said it was on the way to the tip. Wouldn't even take a dollar for it!"

Lucy nods and offers admiring noises while Mabel rips the paper bag open, revealing Mrs Burrows's custard squares.

"Still your favourite, Jim?" Mabel enquires, and so ensues a discussion that traverses all forms of custard and cream filled baked goods: lamingtons, éclairs, ginger snaps and cream buns. Then they get down to business.

"I'm a real lawyer," Jim explains to Lucy, "But I suffered a stroke at 42, and this is a much healthier existence for me.

I've covered property sales before, but I would feel much happier if you had your own representation. You're single?" he enquires, and Lucy nods.

"What about your parents? Can they hook you up with someone?"

"My Mum is in Scotland, and my Dad lives in Wellington, but he's in Shanghai at the moment, and we're not, you know... that close."

"Okay," Jim says, "I'll give you all the documents to read over, and I suggest you find a lawyer to read over them as well – it's the prudent thing to do."

"And you must promise me you'll never build one of those aluminium conservatory things," Mabel demands. "I want that in the contract."

Lucy very quickly realises how little she knows about buying property. Surveys and land rights and LIMs and building consents all have to be checked by a lawyer, and so Lucy acts as any self-respecting almost twenty-nine-year-old would. She calls her mother back in England and sobs uncontrollably for ten minutes, swearing she is giving up and coming back home to live. And though Daphne Dinsdale loves her daughter dearly, she is a little concerned that Lucy and her trail of books and biscuits and bits and pieces might come back and spread out across her sitting room once again, obscuring its clean lines and soft white leather couches.

And Daphne Dinsdale knows how much her daughter wants this cottage, with a lighthouse thrown into the mix. She had picked up the excitement in her voice when Lucy first called with news of the old lady, Mabel, and her plans to sell it to Lucy – as long as she doesn't build a conservatory. A real excitement bubbled through Lucy's descriptions of the real fireplace and the garden gnomes and boysenberries to make jam with.

Lucy's mum isn't sure about the garden gnomes, but her daughter's enthusiasm is back to levels not seen since before the disastrous marriage and baby business. So she digs deep. She opens her address book with a loud thwack and stabs the New Zealand area code and the rest of the number into her phone, before she changes her mind.

"Get on a plane and get down to the Marlborough Sounds," Daphne demands.

"I'm in China," Lucy's father tries, but Daphne stops him.

"I've asked nothing of you in over twenty years, and Lucy, bless her heart, takes what little you offer without a word of complaint."

"I've sent money," Lucy's father protests, but Daphne won't have it.

"Yes, and now she needs *more* than money. She's buying a house. And a lighthouse."

"A lighthouse?" He sounds bemused.

"Yes. And you are going to help her. You get on your private plane or your jet boat, or whatever it is you have these days, and you go and help her. She needs a lawyer, I think, maybe some advice, but mostly – and you listen to me close Lennon Taylor – she needs a father. Not tomorrow, TODAY. Do you hear me?"

"Yes. I hear you," he says.

"She needs someone there to hold her hand, and I can't do that from over here. So you WILL hold her hand because, so help me god, if you don't man up, your life will not be worth living."

"I'll organise it now," he confirms.

"Good," she replies, and hangs up.

Lennon Taylor taps his pen on his desk pad and watches the second hand tick around the brass clock on the wall by the door. He was always sent into a cold sweat when Daphne lost her temper. When Lucy was a baby, he'd slunk off to work, day after day, in the hopes she would realise New Zealand was just as good as Scotland.

Lennon Taylor liked calm and quiet. She knew that, and so she had made home a war zone, with her loud music and her shouting. She would leave Lucy's toys lying around and refused to clean the toothpaste off the bathroom sink.

But he'd told her from the start his business was in Wellington, that he needed to live in the gateway to Asia, and he would not be moving to the other side of the world. Ever.

He had known she was homesick, but he had thought she'd get a grip on it eventually. He hadn't expected her to leave. Or to take Lucy. He loved Lucy. She was a quiet, careful child and he had been surprised at how much he missed her, how empty the house was when they were gone. But the business was growing and taking up all his time, and he'd never been very comfortable with young children. He had thought about asking her over for a holiday but, without her mother, he wasn't sure how he'd manage. What did he know about young girls, anyway?

Lennon Taylor slides open his desk drawer and lifts out a photo of his daughter in a white tutu, her hair pulled back off her face, her smile radiant, a reflection of her mother's. On the back Lucy's handwriting says she is fifteen, her letter 'i' is dotted with a love heart.

In the weeks leading up to the house settlement, Lucy

returns to the vineyard bunk room. Mabel needs time and space to pack and say goodbye, to both her home and to Robert.

Wine Man, who she now knows as Nick, had given Lucy a cheap rate in return for the odd night cooking and scrubbing up. On Mabel's instruction, Lucy has become a regular at The Lonely Jandal. On her third visit, Lucy had raised the courage to wonder if perhaps Mrs Burrows might see her way clear to perhaps making some yo-yo biscuits. Only if she wanted to – not that Lucy minded – because the fairy cakes and the hedgehog slice were delicious.

"Come on in tomorrow," Mrs Burrows had laughed, and from that day on, yo-yo biscuits were always in the cabinet at The Lonely Jandal. So Lucy has become a permanent fixture in Mrs Burrows's café, and, quickly leading on from that, her heart.

Some mornings Lucy shares The Lonely Jandal with an eclectic mix of locals. On Tuesdays a small vanload of senior citizens arrive from a retirement village in Seddon. They like the cheese rolls and the egg sandwiches. On Wednesdays Lucy always stops and chats with the driver of the Zest bus while he or she waits for their tribe of travellers to fill up on Mrs Burrows's mince and cheese pies and coffee.

On Friday mornings there is a mothers group. Mrs Burrows pulls out two big baskets full of toys and a collection of local mums – and sometimes one or two dads – make the most of someone else's home baking and the opportunity to have a gossip, while their kids accept marshmallows from the secret jar behind Mrs Burrows's counter.

Other times, Lucy is alone.

"Winter, you see," Mrs Burrows explains. "Always quiet, but the summers are positively heaving – you'll never get a seat. We open out back with a bunch of tables, sell ice cream from a cart!" But, to Lucy, last summer seems a long way gone, and the next a long way off.

"You need a good book," Mrs Burrows says one day, having finished the crossword in the *Woman's Weekly* in record time, with Lucy's help. She roots round in a box under the counter. "Here you go, what do you make of Freya North? Never read her, myself."

Lucy was immediately swept away to the Scottish moors, and remained glued to Mrs Burrows's squashy couch for a full day, simply distraught when Sal got the chicken pox, and positively praying that she and Richie would live happily ever after.

"I'm closing up now, Lucy," Mrs Burrows says, finally, having cleaned and tidied and sorted everything she could think of, before running out of things to do. "And you'd better get back to the vineyard before it's so dark you can't tell your head from your tail!" So Lucy reads with speed the last four pages, pressing the just-finished book into Mrs Burrows's hands.

"You have to read it," Lucy cries. The following day, she has to knock on the window of The Lonely Jandal to get Mrs Burrows to open the door.

"I may have to close the café – I can't put it down!" Mrs

Burrows had exclaimed. "Poor Sal and the pox!" she cries, waving the book in the air, and Lucy nods in earnest agreement. "And when you've finished that one, there's more!" Lucy tells her, "I've ordered them on Amazon!"

It is on one of the quiet café days, when Lucy has been roped into helping Mrs Burrows ice gingerbread men with white piped icing and pebble eyes, when she overhears a serious voice asking if he could possibly get an espresso?

She giggles as Mrs Burrows explains the ins and outs of her filter coffee machine, which she picked up at one of those stocktake sales for half price. Lucy chooses yellow and pink pebbles for the gingerbread man's buttons, then glances up to see a man's bewildered expression.

"Dad!" she says.

"Lucy. Thank god," he replies. "Your mother gave me directions, but I wasn't sure I'd find you."

"You've talked to Mum?" Lucy asks.

"Yes, she said you might need some help. Something about buying a house?"

"Go and sit your father down," Mrs Burrows gives Lucy a nudge, "and wipe the icing off your chin," she whispers.

Lennon Taylor takes a seat opposite his daughter and accepts the egg and ham club sandwich and the piece of ginger crunch Mrs Burrows puts in front of him with a polite smile.

"I've been a bit worried," Lucy explains. "All the paperwork, it's a wee bit daunting."

"I've got lawyers who can take care of that, so you don't need to worry."

"I thought you were in China."

"I was," her father smiles and with a slight hesitation, he reaches across the table and squeezes her hand, "But now I'm here. For you."

On August 25th, 2012, Lucy Dinsdale signs on the dotted lines, and Mabel places two heavy black keys in the palm of her hand. The deal is done.

In Picton, Lucy and Mabel wait at the airstrip for the helicopter pilot to complete his checks. Lucy would have liked her father to stay for lunch, but he has a flight to catch to Tokyo that he's already delayed twice – once to iron out a land issue, and then again to make sure he would be here for settlement.

"Just in case something pops up, in case you need me," Lennon Taylor had insisted.

"Better late than never," her mother had said when Lucy called to update her.

"Will you be okay?" Lucy asks Mabel, who nods.

"Can't say I ever thought I'd ride on a helicopter. I'm not sure about those blade things, but it's only twenty minutes and I'm sure your dad will hold my hand!" Lennon Taylor looks a bit flustered when Mabel winks in his direction, and he makes himself busy tapping at the screen of his phone.

"I should probably feel sad," Mabel muses out loud. "If it were Robert who was selling he would be miserable, so I'm quite glad it's me standing here and not him. I'll miss what reminds me of Robert but, m'dear, I mainly feel relief. I'm free now to find me own way. I know you young things have years to do that before you settle down, but I was with Robert from the get-go, so there is a bit o' freedom in followin' me own path."

Lucy stares at the keys in her hand. *Is that what I'm doing? Making my own path?* Mabel enfolds Lucy in a hug that lasts a long time, but ends too quickly all the same.

"You'll be great, love. Off you go now, go *home.*"

Lucy squeezes the keys in her hand. *I am formally the owner of a cob cottage and a small sturdy lighthouse.*

"I have a home." She smiles and hugs her father, whose cheeks tinge pink. He hugs her back.

"Call me if you need anything, money, or... you know, advice." Lennon Taylor pushes a curl back from his daughter's forehead and kisses her gently. "You're just like your mother," he smiles, and then they are gone.

Lucy watches her father help Mabel with her seatbelt, then the rotors increase in speed and sound and the helicopter lifts its occupants into the sky. Lucy watches until the small dot in the sky disappears.

"Right, then," Lucy says to a seagull perched nearby on a metal gate. "Time to go home!"

Chapter Thirty

"Good morning, Cottage," Lucy smiles gleefully, on her first morning in her own home. She retrieves the toaster and kettle she bought the previous day at The Warehouse in Blenheim, while making the most of her father's rental car. Her father was a little concerned that she doesn't have a vehicle of her own, but Lucy doesn't think she needs the financial cost of running a car right now.

And anyway, she has a bicycle. It's an old Rally ten-speed that belonged to Mabel's daughter, Charlotte, many moons ago. It's candy pink and has hardly been used, Charlotte having gone off to boarding school and discovered pink bicycles were '*so* last year'. It has a small basket attached to the front and a carrier over the back wheel.

Ignoring the car yard across the road, Lucy had instead gone into the electronics shop where, behind the over-sized televisions and the double-door fridges, a heavily discounted laptop was on display. The salesman told her it really only did simple stuff, and he suggested perhaps she would like to see the one with a better processing speed that was only a wee bit more expensive. But Lucy had felt a bit sorry for the lonely little laptop, and she quickly decided 'simple stuff' was just what she needed right now.

So Lucy eats toast and licks boysenberry jam from her fingers. She found ten jars, lined up neatly in the cupboard above the fridge, with a recipe on a sheet of floral writing paper taped to the inside of the cupboard door.

"Thank you, Mabel," Lucy says for the hundredth time as she munches happily.

Her simple laptop whirs to life, and Lucy checks her emails and logs into Facebook. It's been a couple of months, and she wonders why she never got around to adding Ethan to her list of friends. But then, he hadn't added her either. In fact, they hadn't had much time for Facebook. *We were too busy in the real world,* Lucy thinks sadly, but she is thankful she doesn't have to change 'Ethan and Lucy are in a relationship', to 'Lucy is single'. That would just be too much to bear.

She hovers over the search box and quickly types in his name. But his settings are private and his profile picture makes her heart ache, so she quickly hits the little x in the right-hand corner and vows to leave well enough alone.

Lucy decides that today is not the day to be sad. It is a day for forward thinking and future possibilities. She sits at the old pine table that Mabel included in the chattels – 'Built for this place, it was, I'd never get it out the door!' Mabel had said the same thing about the bed and the washing machine. And the garden gnomes. Lucy studies her living area. Where once Mabel's floral lounge furniture had filled each space, there now lies a blank canvas, a series of empty gaps begging to be filled.

She sips Earl Grey tea from a purple plastic cup and sets about making a list of all the things she will need. Having never furnished a place in her life, Lucy is a little excited and mildly apprehensive.

"Where do I even start?" she had asked Liz on the phone the night before. "I'd like a bookcase, but I've got no books, and do I buy the non-stick pans or the stainless steel? Do I need one of those fluffy mats that go around the bottom of the toilet?" Liz had insisted she calm down and be practical.

"You'll take a while to work out what you need. So don't get too zip-zappy happy. Visa has a lot to answer for, you know."

"Like the naked woman umbrella stand?" Lucy laughed, remembering the ornate vase Liz had brought at a home and garden show one weekend. The artist had captured, with alarming accuracy, the lust-filled gaze of a lady with a large bosom and wildfire hair. It had roamed the rooms of their flat for weeks before settling by the front door, where it regularly amused their friends and shocked the retired conservatives who lived next door.

"Don't be surprised," Liz laughed, "if you wake up with the busty fire-woman vase on your doorstep one morning!"

Following Liz's advice, Lucy decides to start small. She zips up her puffer jacket, dons woolly gloves and cycles into town with Charlotte's old bike helmet snug on her head.

The op shop isn't open, but peering through the windows, Lucy spies a dusty old couch, a small square television and a stack of nesting tables she thinks she might like to have. The sign says they opened at ten, which gives Lucy an hour to fill. She leans her bicycle up against the back of a bench seat and mooches through the magazines in the gift-slash-book shop. She sniffs the scented candles on the shelf beside the counter and purchases postcards from the woman at the cash register, who seems more than a little annoyed to be pulled away from her *Woman's Weekly*.

Lucy jaywalks across the quiet street and settles into one of the squishy couches beside the fire in The Lonely Jandal.

"Morning Lighthouse-Lucy," Mrs Burrows says. "Are you all settled in?"

"First night last night," Lucy smiles. "It's all a bit odd."

"You'll be right as rain. Don't get up, love, I'll bring you a pot of tea."

Lucy waits while Mrs Burrows fusses about finding the flowery teapot that Lucy has mentioned is her favourite.

"Here's your pot, pet." Mrs Burrows sits down opposite Lucy, with her own mug of coffee and a book.

Lucy fills out the postcards she has just bought. She writes to her mum and Liz in England, and to her dad and Georgie in Wellington. She hesitates over the fifth and final one.

"I bought a lighthouse," she writes. Turning the postcard over in her hand, she stares at the photo of baby lambs and daffodils. Lucy sighs.

"*Pillow Talk* is my new favourite," Mrs Burrows says, putting her bookmark in place and drinking back her coffee. "I've just seen on her internet page that there's a new one coming out next year. *Rumours* it's called. Can we pre-order it on the Amazons?" Mrs Burrows asks, Lucy having brought her laptop into the café the week before to show her what 'the Amazons' was all about.

"I already have!" Lucy says.

"Excellent work, young lady," Mrs Burrows nods, pushing up the sleeve of her grey woollen cardigan and twisting the wristband of her watch around so she can see the time. "Now, you better skedaddle. I've just seen Mark and Joy opening up the Bric-a-Brac, so go have a nosey – they've some nice things in there. And I can't be having any distractions today. I'm to make the scones and sandwiches for Justine Brenner's funeral afternoon tea, so I better hop to it."

Lucy leaves Mrs Burrows peeling boiled eggs. She stops back in at the gift-slash-book shop for stamps, and sticks them onto four of the five postcards she has written. She pushes them into the post box.

Mark and Joy seem truly pleased to see a customer, and while Mark disappears out the back to 'sand something', Joy sits on a stool behind the counter, every now and then looking up from her cross-stitch to point things out.

"Couch came from Wendy and Willie – they're up at the orchard. Went on a cruise and came back wanting something *Eye-talian*. They have a couple of cats – are you allergic?" Lucy assures Joy she is not and, bouncing on the two-seater couch a little, she decides it will do nicely. Even if it is pink.

"I'll throw in the lamp," Joy offers, "since they came in together," and Lucy nods and smiles widely at the large standard lamp with the pink tasselled shade.

"We've got one just like it," Joy says, "very stylish," and Lucy nods even more.

"It's quite something," she squeaks, having trouble containing herself.

She definitely wants the nesting tables, and comes across a beautiful full-length pine mirror. She straightens her back, unable to resist standing in ballet second to complete a couple of pliés.

"You're a dancer?" Joy asks over the top of her gold-framed glasses.

"Was a dancer," Lucy replies.

"Any good?" Joy asks.

"I s'pose so," Lucy shrugs.

"Ballet teacher in Seddon shifted to Noosa last year. Noosa is in Australia, just next door to New Zealand," Joy explains, and Lucy smiles again, choosing one white and one sunny yellow tablecloth.

"Could you teach?" Joy asks.

"I did, for a while, in Wellington, and in London," Lucy says, coming back to the counter with a set of chunky coffee mugs and a stack of house and garden magazines.

"Well, what else will you do round here?" Joy asks. "You don't look much of the farming type and you can't be sitting in Mrs Burrows' café for the rest of your life. You know, you wouldn't have to go to Seddon – they can come to us, for a change! Just set up in the church hall. Not on Fridays, mind – they're for the Lions and the Women's Institute."

"Right," says Lucy, plastering a smile across her face.

"She's a total bossy britches," Lucy giggles on the phone to Georgie that night. "But just as I was about to tell her I was actually helping Nick out at the vineyard, and that I had plans for the lighthouse, to have tour groups come for scones and jam and cups of tea, and that she could mind her own beeswax, she and her husband insisted on loading up their van with my couch and things and then they even helped drag them inside! I had to give up a jar of Mabel's jam as a thank you, but, you know what? I'm snug as a bug with a couch and a rug."

"Bloody brilliant!" Georgie says. "And I'm stuck in man-cave hell, trying to convince Chris that we don't need another PlayStation to go with the Xbox and the Wii – isn't that right, you big old nerd?" Georgie calls to Chris, and Lucy stretches out on her couch and giggles.

"So you two are still in *lurve*?" she asks.

"Well, I'm still deciding," Georgie replies, "but I've told him just because I shifted in here doesn't mean we're going to be all smug and married like James and Fran. Both send their love, by the way."

"Send mine back," Lucy grins. "Are they up the duff yet?"

"Not yet, but going at it like rabbits," Georgie replies.

There is a small silence.

"He's doing okay," Georgie adds, without Lucy asking. "Still in Dubai, living like a king apparently, but I think he pretty much spends ninety per cent of his time working, and the other ten per cent posting fuck-off fancy photos on Facebook to make us all jealous."

Lucy flicks at the fringing on the lamp. *But Georgie, does he talk about me? Does he mention my name? Has he asked how I am? Have you told him about the lighthouse?*

"Are you okay, babe?" Georgie asks, "I didn't upset you, did

I?"

"It's fine. You know, I'm fine," Lucy says. "C'est la vie."

The silence returns, as both girls consider how to shuffle the conversation on.

"She's right, you know."

"Who?"

"The bossy bitch from the op shop," Georgie says. "She's right – you should start dance classes. I know you want to do the lighthouse lunches, but that's just on Saturdays, and not till the summer. You'll have to work eventually. So why not?"

Chapter Thirty-One

The windows and doors of the little lighthouse cottage are flung wide open. Lucy munches on cheese and pickle sandwiches, while her feet, clad in thick socks, slide ballet steps under the old pine table. Though it's now January, and the summer sun is at its fiercest, Lucy has invested in a drawer full of white padded sports socks that she uses to slide around the stone floors of her little cottage – simply because it's fun, and because she can.

It's Friday lunchtime, and Lucy has no ballet classes to teach. With help from Joy at the Bric-a-Brac, Lucy has leased the small church hall. From Monday to Wednesday she takes classes from half past three in the afternoon until six in the evening. Joy's husband found her some wall mirrors in a salvage shop in Blenheim and sanded back the frames. With a lick of varnish added, they look brand new.

Her favourite group comes on Thursday mornings for an easy stretch and move session, the older folks mixing with the mothers and babies, learning basic steps and stretches. They finish off with a boogie to Abba or the Bee Gees or a bit of Michael Jackson. She takes requests, and every now and then she will play a bit of Westlife, which reminds her of Fritzi and makes her smile.

Lucy drains the last of her boysenberry and lemon cordial, a recipe she found on the internet and spent the weeks over

Christmas and New Year perfecting, with the help of some good friends. Her first summertime Christmas has been spent with Fritzi, Tom and Georgie, who came without Chris, as he had worked through the holidays.

Her friends brought Monopoly and Scrabble and a small gas barbecue. They ate sausages wrapped in bread and smothered in tomato sauce, and they drank medium wine from a cask in the fridge.

They walked the beach in the sunshine and the rain. They peered through the windows of The Lonely Jandal, and Lucy was a little sad that Mrs Burrows was closed over the Christmas break, right when she was so desperate to introduce her friends.

Fritzi and Tom then headed off in search of fruit picking employment, and Georgie had returned home. Mrs Burrows came back from her Christmas break, having caught up with Mabel in Wellington, checked out her spa bath and been thoroughly shocked that Mabel ordered her groceries off the internet.

"Can you believe it, Lucy? When the supermarket's less than a fifteen minute stroll up the road!"

Then two weeks ago, just as Mrs Burrows had said they would, the tourists had arrived with their jandals and their ice cream money, and Lucy had exchanged her couch inside The Lonely Jandal for a chair under a colourful umbrella outside.

Lucy usually works hard to get to The Lonely Jandal before nine-thirty in the morning, when the sun is warm but there are still spare seats. But today she chooses to take her Cornflakes back to bed, to re-read the proper letter that Liz has handwritten and sent from London – four pages, front and back.

When she gets up, Lucy traipses back and forth to the garden with a blanket, a sun hat, sun block, a magazine and a glass of water. Finally, she settles down beside Gnomeo and Juliet and whiles away the summer morning.

At lunchtime Lucy smothers another layer of beetroot relish on a piece of bread and decides she has been lazy enough. She plans her afternoon - a short bicycle trip into the village for milk and tea bags. An ice cream from Mrs Burrows, vanilla with a chocolate dip, which she insists on paying for. Lucy delights in the skirmish that follows as Mrs Burrows tries to stop her paying.

"I bought a lighthouse."Lucy reads aloud the dog-eared postcard she finds in her tote bag while she is looking for a serviette to wipe the chocolate off her chin. She pops into the book-slash-gift shop, purchases a stamp and stuffs the card in the post box as if it isn't that important. Lucy cycles home under the fierce summer sun.

Two weeks later, Lucy borrows Mrs Burrows's car, a zippy little Toyota Echo, and drives to Kaikoura. She sits on the seashore, slurping a lime milkshake and running her hands over the smooth rocks. She dips her toes in and out of the sea and tells herself she isn't there to take her mind off anything. She watches the tourists take photos on the beach and chooses to think about nothing in particular.

She knows Ethan will have the postcard, but she hears nothing. He doesn't email. He doesn't call. And she pretends it doesn't matter.

Chapter Thirty-Two

Ethan drags a large rubbish bin over to his desk and slowly sorts through every piece of paper, every file he has kept in the last six months. He has already cleared the files from his desktop computer and returned his work laptop and both cell phones.

It is February 1st and, in less than a week, Ethan will be back home. He'll make it just in time for the end of the cricket season. He will be 'of no fixed abode', Georgie having given up the lease on the little house on the hill when she shifted in with Chris. But he's not bothered. Jamie and Fran have offered their spare bedroom for as long as he needs it. He has two promising employment options on the horizon, both with small firms who specialise in building eco-homes. Ethan has discovered that when it comes to project management, bigger is not always better.

This did not come as a sudden discovery for Ethan; rather, a number of small occurrences have combined to help him see the light. Had those things not happened, Ethan may still have been sitting in his fully-furnished apartment on the thirty-eighth floor of a nondescript apartment building in Dubai. A young, single man, making the most of an excellent salary. Not a bad package.

For the last three months, Ethan has travelled with Braunstein to fabulous cities in Asia and America and

Europe. He has met some very rich people, who want Aquiro to take their money and turn it into structures that are bigger and better than what the other rich people have.

Braunstein was impressed with Ethan's work ethic. Ethan didn't get waylaid or distracted in the same way many of his co-workers seemed to. Braunstein thought that perhaps he had found his protégé.

Rather than go out drinking, Ethan worked late nights and weekends to see his projects through to completion. Braunstein had thrown more at Ethan than most and, without complaint, Ethan had set about making things happen. It was impressive to watch, and so Braunstein had decided to mentor the young man, and had high hopes for his future with Aquiro. It was Braunstein's offer that had first jolted Ethan, and made him consider his options.

"I'm moving to the Kuala Lumpur office," Braunstein had said, over coffee and pastries on a quiet Saturday morning. They were less than a week back from the New Year break. "There's a situation that needs some management," he'd continued, sitting upright, as he always did, with arms stretched forward, both hands in fists, resting on his knees. "I'd like you to work another six months here, then come to KL. Six months in Asia, then back here to Dubai – at a higher level, of course – or perhaps Russia. There are some very lucrative contracts on the books that you could sink your teeth into."

Bloody hell, Ethan had thought, as he returned to his desk. *Russia.* Ethan googled Moscow. *Bloody hell*, he thought again when he read that the winter temperatures drop to minus ten degrees. *'Mild' if it climbs over zero degrees?* Ethan's calendar was flashing all kinds of urgent red, so he closed the browser and got back to work.

That weekend he had joined the Braunstein's for a farewell barbecue at their house, which was a series of well-stacked boxes by that point. Benjamin Braunstein's wife was a picture of calm, equipped with a well-worn red clipboard and a serene smile that never wavered, as she directed the caterers to set up the lunch buffet, while instructing the men from the moving company to start with the children's rooms.

"Is it unsettling?" Ethan had asked, "the moving about?" Jodie had laughed, ticking something off her list.

"I don't think about it much, now, to tell you the truth. It's always been part of who we are." She paused to ask one of the passing catering assistants to please refill the punch. "It was harder when the boys were small. It's a logistical nightmare trying to pack and unpack with them underfoot. But now they're at boarding school in England, it's a breeze."

"Do they mind?" Ethan had wondered.

"They hardly notice!" Jodie had laughed, offering to top up Ethan's glass of punch. They joined the other guests on the balcony. "Their rooms are packed and unpacked exactly the same, wherever we are, so they call from school and say 'where are we now'? It's a bit of joke for us, isn't it, Ben?" Jodie gives her husband a squeeze around the waist.

"The kids say 'Kuala Lumpur, have we lived there before?' And we say, 'check your passport'!"

Ethan laughs along, but a small part of him is thankful for the easy, carefree Kiwi childhood he had had. Riding his bike to the beach in summer, camping at Lake Taupo, hanging out with his mates outside the fish and chip shop while their dads were all inside waiting for their orders. Isn't that how he had always imagined his own life would be?

That night Ethan had two whiskies and watched golf till three in the morning, but he had still been unable to sleep.

It was around the same time that Ethan got tired of his *Lonely Planet* guide. There were things he hadn't seen, but the urge to venture out on Sunday afternoons had disappeared. His Facebook status remained suspiciously quiet – so much so that Georgie, his mum, Jamie, and even a girl he'd sat next to in seventh form Chemistry, all sent similar *'is everything okay?'* messages. He had responded by assuring them he was fine, just a little busy.

And then the email arrived. It had been sent by Maia and Gary, who were the owners of the house he had seen through to completion just before his move to Dubai. He hovered his mouse for a moment over the subject line:

Another wee project for you...

Why the hesitation? Ethan asks himself. *What's the problem? There are no 'problems', only 'situations'.* He'd laughed out loud at his own joke. He opened the message and by the final line he had been in no doubt about what he needed to do. What he *wanted* to do.

I want to go home.

"I'm glad I came," Ethan had told his mum that night, "but I'm ready to come back home now."

"It's great here," he had told Georgie on the next phone call, "an incredible experience and one I would have always wondered about if I hadn't given it a go."

"But you're giving up a lot," Jamie had said when Ethan called with the news. "Bloody hell, ten or fifteen years and you could retire with enough money to buy New Zealand."

"But I don't want this life," Ethan explained. "It's just not me. I just don't feel like *me.*"

Ethan wants to connect with his clients, to find out who they are, to have his work be meaningful to someone. Maia and Gary love their house, the home he helped create for them – so much so that they want him to do it again, this time in the Bay of Islands on a strip of land they've purchased for a holiday home. Ethan had realised that this means more to him than all of the many dollars that have been accumulating in his bank account this last six months.

"It's as much about the journey as the end result," Ethan tried to explain to Braunstein, who had called him in to try and convince him to stay at Aquiro.

"You'll regret it, son," Braunstein had said. "You're passing up a once-in-a-lifer."

"I know," Ethan had told him, "and I'm grateful for all your guidance, but I just think I need to forge out my own path. Back home. It's where I belong."

Ethan's desk is clear. His stationery has been returned. He

has filed the last of his paperwork with Human Resources. He has enjoyed a slice of the cake he bought to share with the girls at reception.

He returns to his cubicle to collect his jacket and bag, and there, on the clean desk lies a small stack of letters – mostly junk mail, but on top rests a small cardboard rectangle. He stares at the lambs and the yellow daffodils on the front, then flips it over. The familiar handwriting makes his brow crease. He stands for a long time, unable to move.

"You right there, Ethan?" someone asks.

"Sure," Ethan replies, "I'm fine." But he doesn't looking up from the postcard in his hand.

Then he's gone.

"**He**'s coming back," Georgie tells Liz. It's early on Saturday morning and she is walking to the gym. Chris would tell her to mind her own business, but she has not spoken to Liz since Ethan and Lucy broke up, and she thinks *maybe, with a nudge in the right direction...*

"If only he knew, about CJ and the baby, surely he'd understand. They could work it out." Georgie says, stopping at the dairy for a bottle of water.

"He knows," Liz admits. "I sent him an email."

"Oh my god, when?" Georgie asks, slinging a bunch of change on the counter.

"I know you said he wouldn't talk about it," Liz says, "that he wouldn't talk about Lucy to anyone. And Lucy refused to believe that he would give her the time of day – she convinced herself that he would hang up before she managed two words. So I emailed him. Figured I'd lay out the facts for him. Let him decide what to do from there. Please don't tell Lucy, she'd kill me."

"But what did he say? Did he reply?" Georgie asks, power-walking across the road with her phone pressed to her ear, her water bottle swinging from her other arm.

"I got a very polite reply saying 'thank you for telling me'."

"When?" Georgie demands. "When was this?"

"Christmas," Liz admits sadly.

"Bloody hell." Georgie stops by a lamppost to catch her breath.

"I know," Liz says, "so I guess it's up to him, now."

"Maybe," Georgie replies, "but there's one more person who might be able to help."

Fritzi meets Georgie at the waterfront bar, with only a few minutes to spare before the quiz is due to start. It is Waitangi weekend, and a perfect Wellington day; the sea breeze is light and the sun is still shining brightly at seven in the evening. Fritzi is feeling no pain – a crown of daisy chains has been laid haphazardly on her head.

"Which is he?" she asks Georgie.

"He's not here," Georgie says. "And you're pissed."

"I am very pissed." Fritzi smiles, plopping herself down on a chair. "Now introduce me to these people."

Jamie and Fran shake hands with the pretty German girl and her American boyfriend, who disappears to find more beer.

"I like him," Jamie states, "I must go find more beer too!"

"That's him," Georgie says, grabbing Fritzi's arm. "Oh fuck it, maybe this wasn't such a good idea."

"It is great idea!" Fritzi says, and is off her chair and pushing her way through the crowd before Georgie can stop her.

"Does Fritzi know Ethan?" Chris asks, putting a pint of cider down in front of Georgie and looking into the crowd, where Fritzi has dragged Ethan to a corner and is speaking into his ear.

"Not exactly," Georgie replies, and the crowd closes in so that Fritzi and Ethan are lost from view briefly, before re-emerging beside them.

"Ethan, man, great to have you back, when did you get in?" Chris pumps Ethan's hand.

"Couple of days ago, jet lag's a killer."

He kisses Georgie on the cheek and hugs her tightly. "You," Ethan says, "I've missed you so much. Your gentle caring ways, your cute smile, your charming manners..."

"Get off me," Georgie says, pushing him away.

"I see you've met Fritzi," Georgie nods across the table to where the blonde and her boyfriend are snogging happily.

"Get a room!" she calls to them, and Fritzi simply raises one finger back at her.

The quiz takes their attention for the following hour, and their good-humoured arguing and jostling grows in volume. They dance to The Exponents and Crowded House, telling each other how much they love the Kiwi classics, then they spill out at closing time, welcoming the cool sea breeze and the fresh air.

"I am going to my hostel now," Fritzi informs the group. "But you, Ethan," she scolds, wagging her finger in his direction. He is swaying ever so slightly. His mop of hair, in need of a trim, is damp with sweat. He smiles and nods at Fritzi.

"She is very beautiful, on the insides and the out. If I wasn't in love with the man now," Fritzi waves an arm towards Tom, "I would be taking the woman Lucy any day."

"Time to go," Tom says, putting an arm around his girlfriend and kissing her forehead. "I would apologise for her outspokenness," he smiles at Ethan, "but she's usually right about these things." And with a round of handshakes, the rest of the group watch as Tom and Fritzi stumble their way up the road to their hostel.

"Well then," Ethan says, "I think it's time to go home."

Chapter Thirty-Three

Lucy stands frozen by the window as the car comes closer, winding up the driveway that leads to her cottage. The crunch of tyres on gravel moves her, but only in a circle. Where should she go? What should she do? She twists the tassels on her pink scarf and jiggles one foot.

He isn't a shuffler. His feet fall in regular solid crunches that she counts. *Six, seven, eight,* then silence. Someone laughs quietly in the kitchen on the morning talk-back radio. "Shhh," she implores them.

She waits for a knock on the door, knows he is standing on the other side. Instead, she hears a muffled voice.

"I saw you at the window, are you going to let me in?"

A nervous giggle escapes and her eyes fill with tears that she tries to blink quickly away. Her feet carry her forward and her hand rests on the big iron handle. She pulls the heavy door.

Lucy smiles at the man on her welcome mat and he smiles back. He's the same. Day-old stubble and faded blue jeans. Scuffed sneakers that were white last time she saw them. The jacket is new, but the scarf is the one they found at the Underground Market.

"I see you got yourself a place," he says. She smiles at the shiny silver zip on his jacket. "Bloody shocking weather, mind you."

"Do you want to come in?" she asks, standing back to let him through.

"Nope! I wanna see the big one." Ethan raises his eyebrows up towards the lighthouse, and then he's gone, disappearing around the corner of the cottage and up the path beyond the boysenberries.

Lucy grabs her jacket off the hook behind the door and hurries up the path to the lighthouse. She can see him, already leaning up against the wobbly old stone wall.

"So you chose a lighthouse, eh?" He doesn't take his eyes off the stumpy white turret squatting before them. "I thought it would be taller."

Lucy rests beside him.

"It lost its top in 1952. Big storm. Robert, the man who restored it, he only got this far… but I like it like this." Lucy shrugs, "And I promised Mabel. It came with the cottage. She's gone on a cruise, Mabel has, and she had to have her knees done, and the money was there, from my father." She's talking too much and she can't seem to find the off switch. But Ethan doesn't stop her, he simply nods along.

"I always wanted a place by the sea, and what could be better than a lighthouse?" she carries on.

"Two lighthouses?" Ethan keeps his gaze on the clouds moving quickly above them, but she feels the gentle nudge of his elbow and can see a smile playing at the corner of his mouth.

They stand a while longer. Shoulder to shoulder, heads turned up to the sky.

Lucy is the first to move. She opens the small, heavy door at the base of the lighthouse,

"Come inside?" she asks. The empty cylinder rises around them; its bare space echoes his voice.

"It's empty," he says, stating the obvious.

"Waiting for a plan," she replies, chewing her lip. Now he is here, he is filling up the empty spaces, as she knew he would. He's pacing its width, head tilted left and upwards; the back of his fingers rub back and forth on his chin. Lucy scrunches her toes in her own scuffed sneakers, willing herself to wait patiently.

Ethan comes and stands beside her, hands stuffed in pockets, neck still stretched upwards.

"A grand design," he smiles, "But what to do with it. I wonder what Kevin McCloud would say?"

"He'd say, 'why didn't you think about that before you bought a ruddy lighthouse?'" Lucy replies, and their laughter echoes around them.

"A lot of work," he muses, "but it could be magnificent."

"Hmmm," she says.

Two imaginations twist and entwine in peaceful silence, until the wind whips through the open door, rattling the teacups, knocking over the toast rack and blowing the morning newspapers across the table. Except there is no table. No toast and no teacups.

"Rather not do it alone," she whispers into her pink scarf. He doesn't hear her. Ethan is captivated with a beam of light that cuts across the lighthouse. It enters through a window up high and escapes from one below. She mumbles something that makes no sense. Words that do not form a sentence.

"What was that?" he says, scrunching up his nose the way she loves. But she doesn't see it.

She's gone.

Fortifying breaths of salty air. He comes and stands behind her, not quite touching. The sea is rough today.

"It's like a washing machine," she comments.

"We're stuck on the spin cycle," he answers. He rests his chin on her head and she aches to melt into him, but stuffs her hands into her pockets instead. A boat lurches round the corner of the bay. The wind whirls around them as they watch the boat navigate the white soapy waves. Its progress is slow, but neither of them have anywhere else to be.

"I wish you hadn't come," she whispers into a particularly blustery gust of wind.

She doesn't mean it and he doesn't believe her. He turns her around, the boat forgotten.

"A postcard?" he asks, holding her firmly. "You run away and months later, I get a postcard with one line on it?"

"I didn't run away."

"You did. I came home that day and it was like you'd never been there. Like you'd tried to erase us," Ethan says.

"I thought you were with her. Sharon." Lucy barely whispers the name.

"I wasn't."

"I know that now, but I watched you on the street. She was

all over you."

"Exactly, *she* was all over *me*."

"I know."

"And then your husband called."

"*Ex*-husband. Not even that really."

"I know that now. But I thought at least you'd come and explain."

"You were so mad, I thought you didn't... you know... anymore."

"I didn't, for a long time. I mean come on Lucy, a husband?"

"Not a real one."

"But he was a real one." He's in her face, but she can't look at him, so she rests her forehead on his chest and inhales the scent of washing powder.

"I'm sorry," she mumbles. He doesn't answer and she doesn't expect him to.

"I just... I didn't plan... I thought, I didn't know he'd call. I wanted you. It's just... *we* happened and it was all so fast and you said you loved me and I didn't want to ruin it, and then I did anyway."

Lucy takes a step away from Ethan, concentrates hard on the dirt beneath her feet.

"I was pregnant. Before I came to New Zealand."

"I know," Ethan says, shoving his own hands in his pockets.

"I lost the baby, but we were married by then."

Ethan takes a step closer and whispers in her ear, "I know," but Lucy has to keep talking.

"I knew we'd made a mistake, but I didn't know what to do.

So I figured we'd give it a go. It was easier, you know, than not staying."

"I know."

"Then I found out he was, um, not monogamous."

A fancy phrase for a dirty cheating bastard, Ethan thinks.

"So I left," Lucy continues.

"I know." Ethan gives her a little shake. "I *know*."

"You know?" Lucy says.

"Your friend Liz. Don't be mad."

"You know." Lucy is trying hard to process this information in time and space.

"Yes. And then I got your postcard. *'I bought a lighthouse.'* That's all you could write, after everything?"

"I thought you were probably with her. In Dubai."

"I wasn't."

"I know," Lucy says, "Georgie called me on Waitangi Day. Drunk as a skunk. Told me you came back."

"I came home," Ethan confirms, reaching out for a hand to hold.

"And here you are."

"Here I am."

"I'm cold."

"So am I."

Lucy and Ethan sit in weary silence at The Lonely Jandal. The rain thrums on the roof above them, the sun umbrellas are folded down outside, the tourists are few and far between. Mrs Burrows bustles around their table, telling them it's just a passing storm, that there is plenty of summer sunshine yet to be had.

"Don't be fooled into thinking you can put away your sun hats – this time next week we'll be wheeling out the barbecue again!" Mrs Burrows plonks down a teapot and two china teacups. Lucy and Ethan watch as she disappears behind the counter, then returns to present each of them with a fancy china plate, pink roses for her, blue diamonds for him. Each holds a yo-yo biscuit.

"Your favourite," Ethan smiles at Lucy.

"She's *my* favourite," Mrs Burrows says, her cheeks flushing a little. "But we haven't seen you before." A little accusation hangs in the air. "She was ever so quiet. Only just bringing her out of her shell." Mrs Burrows explains.. Lucy's cheeks flush and she stares at her dainty silver teaspoon.

"We've been apart a while." Ethan says. "She had a husband." There is a serious tone to his voice, and Lucy glances up, then quickly returns to her spoon. She can pick the twinkle in his eye.

"He had a *Shazza!*" Lucy volleys back. Mrs Burrows puts her hands on her heart, and glares at the pair of them. She takes back her yo-yos and hovers, a plate in each hand.

"Do you still have a husband?" she demands of Lucy.

"Definitely not," Lucy shakes her head.

"And you. Do you still have a... a Shazza?"

"No, I most definitely do not," Ethan says, and gives Lucy's foot a small nudge under the table.

"So are you a favourite?" Mrs Burrows asks Ethan.

"Favourite what?" he asks.

"A favourite of Lucy's."

"I hope so," Ethan smiles at Lucy, who feels her cheeks burning. Mrs Burrows seems pleased.

"I like a bit of romance," she says, and sets down the yo-yos. "I best be getting back to the lolly cake. Amy Farley is having her fifth birthday here tomorrow.

Mrs Burrows busies herself straightening the salt and pepper shakers on the other tables.

"You know, we've never had a wedding here before," she sings out from behind the kitchen door.

Epilogue

Lucy stands on the beach and lets her heels sink into the stony sand as the tide washes over her feet. She has spent the better part of the early morning clambering up and down a ladder, attaching bunting to the white walls of her lighthouse. She turns now, to watch the bright red and navy blue flags flutter in the breeze.

The beach is my happy place, Lucy thinks. But it's just gone ten and she's a bag of nerves.

Lucy checks the time on her cell phone. Ethan was leaving Auckland on the first flight at six in the morning, changing planes in Wellington at quarter to eight.

He should be back soon. She smiles, enjoying the anticipation of seeing him again after a week apart.

Lucy loves that Ethan is so passionate about his work. It's a year since his return, and Ethan has put together a small team of experts. Their enviro-homes are attracting attention from all over New Zealand, as well as Australia and Asia. Their focus on environmentally-friendly building products and techniques even has them up for a couple of awards. And although Ethan is busier than ever, he is home every weekend and at least one full week every month.

Lucy smiles as her phone buzzes to life in her hand. She quickly follows the path back up to the lighthouse, and sets about unstacking white plastic chairs, placing them in neat rows.

"Looks bloody great!" Ethan says, pushing his sunglasses up onto his head. "Where the bloody hell is everyone?" Lucy drops the chair she is holding and grabs her husband in a long, tight hug.

"The young ones stayed at the vineyard last night. The oldies are coming on buses at two, from motels in Seddon. Do you think it'll work?" Lucy waves her arms at the chairs, then up at the bunting. "I won't put the flowers out till just before the guests arrive. I've got a load of bubble mixture for the kids, and the champagne is chilling for the toast straight after the ceremony."

"It'll be amazing," Ethan says, kissing his wife gently on the lips. He thinks back to their own wedding on the beach in Rarotonga. The rain had held off just long enough for them to slip on their rings, and they had joined their friends, running for shelter under the large palm trees. They had kissed in the rain, as husband and wife, and when the clouds parted they had danced the night away.

"The caterers are due at midday," Lucy broke into his thoughts. "Georgie found out that Wendy is a whiz with nails, so she's gone up to the orchard for an hour. She's the most relaxed bride you've ever seen. She keeps smiling at me and saying 'It's not raining.' I think she might have taken something. Oh – Mrs Burrows! Don't let me forget, she'll be here in half an hour with the cake."

"So we've got thirty minutes?" Ethan asks.

"Yes, but the marquee isn't ready for the caterers and the cake table's not set up."

"But for the next half hour," Ethan says, undoing the tie at the top of her sundress and pushing her gently back towards the lighthouse, "we've got the place to ourselves?"

"I think so," Lucy murmurs, and lets him cover her mouth with his own. She is helpless to stop her hands travelling under his T-shirt.

"Half an hour," Ethan says, "I can work with that. And, Lighthouse-Lucy, I have it on very good authority that weddings make you very horny."

Mrs Burrows arrives early. There is no one in the marquee, though Gnomeo and Juliet are watching over their garden as they swing gently from the pohutukawa tree.

At the cottage, Mrs Burrows finds the doors and windows thrown open, and she taps her foot and shimmies along as Michael Bublé croons from the radio. She gets halfway up the path to the lighthouse, but is stopped in her tracks by the sound of laughter and the sight of two sets of bare legs revealed as the lighthouse door blows slightly open. She turns quickly, not wanting to see any more than she already has.

Mrs Burrows returns to the marquee and once the cake is displayed, she pops round to the back of the garden.

"I'm not one to gossip," Mrs Burrows tells Gnomeo and Juliet, who blush furiously, "but I do make a fabulous christening cake!"

Made in the USA
Charleston, SC
13 January 2014